TO CATCH
A LORELEI

Phyllis Houseman

A KISMET™ Romance

METEOR PUBLISHING CORPORATION
Bensalem, Pennsylvania

KISMET™ is a trademark of Meteor Publishing Corporation

First Printing November 1991.

ISBN: 1-878702-65-3

Again, to my only hero, Jack.

To Valerie and Daniel, for keeping their
mother up-to-date.

To my best fans in Florida, Mom and Dad and Susan.

To Kate and Nalini, who really cared.

And to Sue, whose friendship is steadfast
and treasured.

PHYLLIS HOUSEMAN

The hero and heroine in Phyllis's books fall in love
very quickly, just as she did with her husband, Jack
. . . when they were eight years old. Unfortunately,
Fate then kept them apart for years. During this time,
Phyllis studied biology, was a Peace Corps Volunteer
in Ecuador, and taught high school in Detroit. But
when she met Jack again, they became engaged on
their third date. After marrying and having a daughter and son, they moved to California, where they
live in a suburb northeast of San Francisco.

PROLOGUE

There was a minute's silence after the tenth ring, but then the phone began ringing again. The insistent noise finally destroyed Daniel Logan's concentration on the work he was doing at his drafting table. Running strong fingers through his dark auburn hair, Daniel gave the clamoring instrument a blistering stare that should have melted it down. However, when the phone didn't become smoking slag, or even stop ringing, the tall, powerfully built man vented some steam by throwing his drawing pencil at the device.

Glancing at his watch, he decided that only one person would be calling him at ten-thirty at night—his agent, the very persistent Sherman Schreiber. Sighing deeply, Daniel slid off his perch on the high stool and advanced toward the phone.

"What do you want, Sherman?" he grumbled into the receiver.

The short pause at the other end was quickly followed by a cheerful, "Dan, my man, how's it going?"

"You know how it's going. Too damned slow. I didn't get back to L.A. from that shoot at Lake Arrowhead until a couple of hours ago. Now I'll probably be up all night

7

getting this project finished for tomorrow. One more assignment like today's, Schreiber, and I'm going to quit modeling, contract or not. You can sue me."

"Now, Dan, don't be angry with me. It was supposed to be a simple two-hour session. I had no way of knowing that it would run on so long. But look at the bright side, twelve hours' pay will go a long way toward your tuition next fall."

"I won't be needing any tuition if I flunk out. I mean it, Sherman. I've already spent more time modeling this semester than I should have, so don't put any more demands on me until I'm finished with finals next Monday."

"I didn't call about another assignment, Dan. I just wanted to check with you about your decision on the Hunt woman."

"Hunt?"

"Yeah, Lorelei Hunt, the lady in San Diego who wrote that terrific fan letter to Anytime Jeans about the ad you did for them. I really think you should reconsider my idea and go on a few dates with her. I guarantee the publicity I generate will put your modeling career over the top."

"Sherman, how many times do I have to tell you that I just don't have time for that publicity nonsense. And as for a long-term career in modeling, you do remember that clause in my contract, don't you? I'm out of the game the minute I have enough money to carry me through a master's degree in architecture."

"Dan . . . Dan! Lord, I'll never understand how you talked me into that clause. But if it's quick money you're after, wouldn't it be wiser to put your studies on hold? Since you started modeling so late, you only have a few years left to make the big bucks. . . ."

Daniel squeezed his eyes shut as Sherman droned on. He had heard this same argument from the man a thousand times in the last three years. And given the work load he had to juggle, maybe his agent had a point. But he hated the idea of dropping out of school; something might keep him from getting started again. Damn it, he was too tired to argue right now.

"Look, Sherm, it's really getting late and I've got hours of work to do," Daniel said into the phone. But his agent just kept talking.

". . . And, Dan, you know that you're right on the edge of being a superstar. Look at the coverage you got on the last few ads. Look at the letters the jeans people got. The one the Hunt woman wrote was the best of the bunch, but there were hundreds more."

Although Daniel wanted to strangle Sherman for keeping him from putting the finishing touches on his semester project, he couldn't help smiling at the mention of those letters. He had read a sampling of the mail forwarded to Sherman. He had been flattered, although some of the notes were so steamy he could have reduced his heating bill to nothing by papering his apartment walls with them.

Lorelei Hunt's letter had been very different from the rest. It had been warm and funny and poetic. Instead of dwelling on his physical characteristics—like the others had—she praised the ad's creativity, and complimented the company on using a tongue-in-cheek approach.

Yet, as much as he'd like to meet the woman who could write such an appealing, perceptive letter, Daniel had to remember his priorities. After a rocky beginning, he finally had his life together. He was back on the track that he had somehow slipped from a decade ago. At twenty-eight, he might be one of the oldest juniors in the Architecture Department, but he certainly had earned the highest grade point average.

No, he had no time for publicity dates. He didn't even have time for real ones, his tense body often reminded him.

"Sherm, absolutely not. I do *not* want to meet Lorelei Hunt, and that's final."

ONE

"Don't tell me that *you're* Lorelei Hunt!" Sherman Schreiber's voice vibrated with shock when his horrified eyes scanned the tall woman's thick glasses, lank hair, and grimy clothing.

"But that's who I am," Lorelei countered, as she stood shivering in the office of her exotic plant nursery. She squeezed out a little moisture from her sweatshirt and then brushed back a strand of water-darkened, pale-blond hair from her glasses. She had been so rushed this morning that she had just grabbed the old hornrims she kept for emergencies instead of putting in her contacts.

"I said don't tell me that!" Schreiber pleaded. And with a groan of despair, he raised his arms to the heavens, in a pose reminiscent of *Fiddler on the Roof*. "I'm sorry, Lord. I swear that I'll never go behind a client's back again. But did you have to punish me like this?"

The agent surveyed Lorelei again, and then suddenly pulled a folded paper from his suit pocket. He shook out the creases and shoved the glossy magazine page into her hands.

10

"Are you really the same person who wrote a fan letter about this ad featuring my client, Daniel Logan?"

Daniel! Ignoring the man's incredible behavior for the moment, Lorelei's direct blue gaze softened to misty aquamarine behind her glasses. "So that's his name . . . Daniel." She attached the biblical label to the male model who had made such an impression on her three months ago.

Lorelei looked down at the ad in her hands, but she really didn't have to examine it to remember each and every nuance of the devastating picture. From the length of the encroaching shadows, it appeared that the photo had been taken at dusk. And in the distance, cirrus clouds veiled jagged peaks with glowing bands of orange and indigo. But dominating the picture—standing on a high, windswept plateau—was a tall, broad-shouldered man, supporting a young mountain lion across his bare back.

Bathed in the sun's last light, the model's golden-brown skin seemed to snare the lingering heat out of the sky to warm his nakedness, covered only by a drum-tight length of denim jeans. The man's body was magnificently powerful; it had to be to hold such a heavy animal without bending in the least.

Draped over the laughing man's shoulders, the huge, amber-toned creature had wrapped its paws and sinuous tail around the strong column of the model's long neck. From the look on its feline face, the wild animal had apparently been tamed into loving submission by the force of Daniel Logan's wide, sensuous smile.

The rest of the man's features hinted at a rare, rugged beauty, but the shadows of sunset played all sorts of visual tricks. Lorelei couldn't tell the color of the thick hair that whipped across a broad, high forehead, or decide if his eyes were light or dark. However, she was left with an overwhelming impression of masculine perfection.

But the impact Daniel Logan's picture had made on Lorelei, in those first awful days after her divorce, hadn't been just because of his heroic body or classic facial features. What had compelled her to save a copy of this ad, and to write the letter, was the powerful message radiating from those laughing eyes.

Lorelei thought that Logan's forceful gaze proclaimed him to be a man in complete charge of his life, a man who needed nobody's support. His cheerful expression also hinted to her that, while he might have a serious objective in life, he had the sense of humor to smile at the fates that required him to pose in such a frivolous way to get to his destination.

Intuitively, Lorelei was sure that he only modeled because it gave him the means to realize his ambition. And having postponed many of her own dreams for long years, she fiercely admired people who could mold their lives to achieve something meaningful. In retrospect, she could even understand her ex-husband's unswerving quest for his heart's desire, though it had made mincemeat of her own.

"Ms. Hunt? MS. HUNT!"

A potent image of man and beast remained etched in her brain, even when Lorelei abruptly handed back the ad. But then she forced herself to focus on the short, beefy person in front of her.

"I'm sorry, Mr. Schreiber, I don't usually wool-gather like that. But today has been one disaster after another. I gave Tom—my manager—the day off to be with his wife and new baby, so I had to do his work as well as mine. And just before you arrived, the overhead sprinkler in the oldest greenhouse decided to disintegrate. As you can see, I got drenched before I could turn it off."

Today it had been the sprinkler. Tomorrow, who knew what else would break down? Without her grandfather and his mechanical expertise, Lorelei had been shelling out money for repairs faster than it came in. Shaking her head, she cast a leery eye out of her office window at the ancient glass structure. The gesture dislodged that wayward hank of hair again. As Lorelei's hand automatically traveled upward to push it out of her eyes, she got a whiff of the manure she had been shoveling from the storage bin when the waterworks began.

"Look, Mr. Schreiber, the retail store opens in half an hour, and I have to change my clothes. San Diego may be in the middle of a heat wave, but my goosebumps haven't read the weather report today," she laughed.

The man didn't respond. He looked at Lorelei with such a sad, lost expression on his face that she suddenly felt sorry for him.

"Oh, Mr. Schreiber, you came all this way for nothing. I thought you understood when we talked last week that I don't want to go out with your client. If you can wait a few minutes until I change, I'll be glad to explain again why I refused your offer. Here, sit down at my desk and look through our catalog of exotic plants."

She gently guided the dazed man by the elbow to her swivel chair.

"As a model's agent, I'm sure you'll appreciate these beautiful specimens, even if they're the rooted variety." But when she put the booklet down on the desk in front of him, Lorelei could see that the man wasn't really listening to her.

He shook his head as if to clear it, consulted his watch, and then muttered, "Nine-thirty . . . he might still be at home. Say, Ms. Hunt, while you're changing, could I use your phone to make a call? It's long distance, but I'll charge it to my account," he promised, giving Lorelei another sweeping scan, which again concentrated on her face.

"Sure, help yourself." She indicated the instrument on her desk. Turning away from him as he began dialing, Lorelei ducked through a low, curtained archway into the short hall that separated her office from the retail shop.

A Formica counter nestled in an alcove of that passageway. As she went by, Lorelei automatically glanced at the mini-refrigerator and hot plate that rested on the smooth surface. She often made a quick lunch for herself here, rather than going up to her apartment on the second floor of the building.

What a gracious hostess you are, not even offering the poor man a cup of coffee, she chided herself. Maybe Howard had been right about that particular failing.

Lorelei quickly remedied her oversight by setting water to boil in a glass pot. She then got a clean mug from an overhead cabinet and spooned some instant coffee into it.

Howard . . . the name buzzed in her brain . . . Dr. Howard Taylor. Lorelei realized that she had made great progress. She hadn't even thought about her former husband in days, not since she'd received the invitation to her tenth-year high school reunion. Attached to that summons had been a sincere little note from Howard's new wife, Carol, urging Lorelei to come to the event. Carol, a former classmate of Lorelei's, had organized the affair.

Howard must be relieved to have an expert taking care of his entertaining now, Lorelei thought ironically. His second wife was in the catering business. And even more important, Carol also had a father who owned a plastic surgery clinic, the same prestigious organization Howard had lusted to join since starting his residency in that field two years ago. Talk about killing two birds with one stone.

"Well, Howard, at least I'll never have to worry about baking sagging souffles or making runny pâté, again," Lorelei muttered, remembering two of the disasters she had concocted in the waning days of their eight-year marriage.

"Dan? Daniel, this is Sherm."

The man in the next room had finally reached his party. And due to some quirk in the acoustics of the old building, the agent's penetrating voice seemed to be speaking right into Lorelei's ear.

"I was just going to hang up, Dan. Were you in the shower? You just got to sleep? Don't tell me that you really did stay up all night on that project! My boy, you'd better stop burning the candle at both ends. You can't afford bags under your eyes in your profession. Hey, watch your language on the long-distance telephone lines. No, I'm not in Los Angeles, I drove down to San Diego early this morning to see that Hunt woman."

In the alcove, Lorelei held her breath. Against her better judgment, she found herself concentrating on every word Sherman Schreiber said to his client.

"Dan . . . Dan! Don't blow up, I'm calling to apologize. I feel so bad about doing this, I didn't even wait till I got back to tell you how sorry I am for going against your wishes. All I can say in my defense is that it seemed like a natural. I just couldn't resist trying to set up some publicity dates for you and the lady. But let me assure you that I agree with you one hundred percent now, it has to be the worst idea I've had all year.

"Yeah, I'll put it to you this way: if I ever caught you cheating with my wife, I wouldn't . . . ah . . . I wouldn't make you sing soprano. Hell, no, I'd lock you up for a year with this dog. That's right, a real mutt. A telephone voice like the siren she was named for, but in person, she's a *matzopunim! Matzopunim* . . . haven't you heard that Yiddish phrase in L.A.? It means being as plain as a piece of matzo . . . you know, that flat cracker bread."

A piece of matzo? Lorelei's eyes flew to the small mirror tacked to the wall above the sink. "Oh, my God!" Well, it was certainly true that she did not look her best.

Not with her hair plastered wetly to her make-up free face, her eyebrows and lashes all but invisible . . . and the glasses . . . the glasses! Lorelei had completely forgotten that the lenses distorted her irises, magnifying them into huge, light blue moons.

Frog Eyes! She resurrected her own teenaged description for the effect the strong prescription lenses had on her eyes. At sixteen, Lorelei had repeated the phrase so often that her parents finally let her buy contacts.

No wonder the agent had been shocked by her appearance, Lorelei decided, while she dimly registered the one-sided conversation going on in the next room. She tried to smile into the mirror, but instead she felt the sudden rush of burning tears and struggled to blink back the acid moisture before it fell.

She knew there were good reasons for not eavesdropping on other people's conversations. The call she had overheard Howard make to Carol, six months ago, should have cured her of that vice.

Lorelei sighed. Maybe this sudden feeling of depression was her own fault, she thought, running her fingers through her wet hair, trying to deal with the mess.

No! Howard's defection had almost destroyed her self-confidence, but Lorelei had been working very hard during the last few months to counteract the damage he had done. And she wasn't going to let anyone undermine her progress, she vowed, as yet another shout of laughter erupted from the next room.

That blind toad! Even at her worst, a model's agent should have been able to see beyond wet hair and a lack of make-up, Lorelei thought defensively. Hadn't she been labeled "The Most Beautiful Girl In The World . . . Or Any Other Planet," in her high school yearbook?

"That man is going to be sorry he ever heard of Lorelei Hunt!" she muttered. She really didn't know if she meant Schreiber or his gorgeous client, Daniel Logan, who must be laughing at her, too.

She angrily pushed the hair back into its original disarray as an idea hatched in her quick brain. Damning both men, Lorelei concocted a deliciously devious plot that would charcoal broil the pair in the flames of her righteous indignation.

"He sees a *matzopunim*, does he? I'm a mutt, am I? Well this is one dog who hasn't had her rabies shots!"

Taking deep breaths, Lorelei calmed herself by focusing her attention on pouring the hot water for the coffee. When she felt ready to initiate her revenge, she picked up the serving platter and re-entered the office, just as Sherman Schreiber cradled the receiver.

"I thought you could use something hot to drink," Lorelei soothed silkily when the man whirled the chair around, a guilty flush on his face.

Seeing that he was ready to bolt for the door, she quickly put the tray down and said, "Look, Mr. Schreiber, I know what a busy man you are, so I won't tie you up any longer. But you'll be happy to know that I've changed my mind. I *will* go on a series of publicity dates with your client . . . ah . . . this Daniel Logan. I wasn't thinking when I turned you down last week. The exposure will be good for my business, which you wisely pointed out in our earlier phone conversation."

Schreiber's mouth had been doing a good imitation of a beached fish all during Lorelei's pronouncement. But as she finished, he finally got his vocal cords working again.

"No! Oh my god, no! Ah . . . that is, Ms. Hunt, I think your first arguments were very logical. You really don't want to leave yourself open to curiosity seekers or . . . or to the threat of obscene phone calls."

The man desperately snatched at two of Lorelei's previous objections. But his rapid sweep of her naked face and manure-covered clothing eloquently expressed his personal opinion that such a call would probably be the highlight of her sex life for the year.

"Well, I was just being overly cautious," Lorelei answered sweetly, not letting her mounting anger crack through her saccharine façade. "Being linked with the country's fastest-rising male model, as you called him, will certainly bring in customers to this nursery. But more importantly, it will also help me publicize my new column in the San Diego *Record* and give me a bigger audience for the book I'm writing."

"Column? Book?"

As a puzzled frown further wrinkled the agent's face, Lorelei wickedly fed the panicked man the ingredients for a perforated ulcer.

"You see, I've been doing articles about exotic plants for a local weekly this past year. And my good friend, Mark Tolliver, suggested to his father, George Tolliver, that I could write the same sort of column for the *Record*, and all the other dailies he owns across the country. Uncle George thought it was a terrific idea, and he also wants me to do a book for his publishing house. It's going to be a guide to help people find and enjoy the interesting and exotic plants we have all over this city. I'm calling it *Blooming San Diego*."

The pun sailed right over the agent's head as Schreiber stuttered, "G-George T-Tolliver? Not . . . *the* George Tolliver?"

"Oh, of course, being an agent, you're aware that he's president and chairman of the board of the Tolliver Publishing Consortium. Anyway, Uncle George said that my articles will help balance all the advertisements he runs in his Sunday magazine."

Lorelei smiled broadly, swooping in for the *coup de grâce*. "You know, ads for cigarettes, and liquor, and clothing. In fact, that's where I first saw Daniel Logan, in a Tolliver Sunday supplement."

"The Tolliver Publishing Consortium . . . Uncle George . . . chairman of the board," Schreiber chanted. "You're really friends with the Tollivers?"

"Mark's probably the best friend I've ever had," Lorelei said.

And that was the absolute truth. In fact, Lorelei didn't know how she could have survived the last few months without Mark. Although he'd been out of town much of the time since her separation and divorce, he had called her several times a week. He was in the Sierra Nevada mountains now, climbing the rugged peaks with the conservation group he all but supported, trying to rescue the fragile eggs of endangered birds. Yet, as tired as he must have been, Mark phoned regularly to check on Lorelei's emotional state, and to chide her about working so hard at the nursery and on her writing projects.

She enjoyed the calls, but for the last week he had ended each conversation with the disquieting reminder that, when he got back into town, he had something very important to tell her. Lorelei fervently hoped he wasn't making plans to marry yet again. Over the years, she had often listened to Mark's troubles when wife number one, and then number two, had made his life hell.

A squeaking floorboard alerted Lorelei that Sherman Schreiber had taken advantage of her distracting thoughts to inch toward the door. "Well, he isn't going to escape from me that easily," Lorelei muttered under her breath, moving between him and freedom.

"As I was saying," she went on as if she had never paused, "Mark's mother and mine went to college together. And they remained bosom buddies, even after

Aunty Jane married into all that money . . . all that power.''

Schreiber froze, and Lorelei had trouble not laughing as she watched his thoughts march across his face. He clearly was weighing the chances of his client, of all his clients, being subtly blackballed by the powerful Tolliver chain.

"Ah, Lorelei, honey. Maybe I can get Daniel to come down here in a week or two. Perhaps a meal in some hidden room . . . er . . . that is, an intimate dinner in an exclusive club would be just the thing for you two, sweetie?''

"Sorry, Sherm, baby, but I also have plans. And if I'm going to get any benefit out of this, I expect the full-boat publicity treatment. World premiers, charity balls, the works. And the first 'date' has to be tomorrow night.''

"But that's impossible! Dan has ah . . . er . . . a commitment on Monday to prepare for, and he'd have my hide if I went back on my word about that stuff. You wouldn't believe the temper the guy has if you cross him," the man mumbled on.

"Tomorrow, Mr. Schreiber. Please don't force me to call Mark . . . or Uncle George. You know, the darling man says I'm just like the daughter he's always wanted. And if anyone ever hurt me . . ." Lorelei let her voice drift off on just the right note of delicate menace.

Schreiber gagged. "OK, OK . . . tomorrow night. Dan's going to kill me, but where should I make your reservations?''

"How about the Hotel Ramona? I've never been there, but Mark's always raving about the place, even though the *paparazzi* swarm in whenever somebody famous is staying there. But that suits our purpose perfectly, doesn't it, Mr. Schreiber? Tomorrow's Saturday, the busiest night of the week for a hotel. We do want Daniel to get maximum exposure, right? And there I'll be, hanging on his arm. A barnacle couldn't stick closer to your client than I will, I can assure you.''

Lorelei demonstrated the technique she would use, linking her arm—soaked sweatshirt and all—with the immaculately attired man. She looked down at him through the screen of wet hair that had fallen across her glasses again.

Smiling sweetly, Lorelei tried to avoid wrinkling her nose as the early morning sun streamed through the office windows. The sunshine highlighted a dancing cloud of dust particles, while it heated the pungent coating on her shirt. As she snuggled next to him, the warmed air carried the earthy aroma of well-rotted manure up into Sherman Schreiber's twitching nostrils.

TWO

"Lorelei, I can't stand it any more! If you don't tell me exactly what's going on . . ." Susan Grant threatened her younger sister with the moist make-up sponge she had been using on Lorelei's face. "Tell me, my dear, or I'll wipe off all my work, and you'll have to meet this man in your beautiful bare skin!"

"All right, all right!" Lorelei laughed. "Help me off with this cape and I'll reveal all, Suzie."

She struggled to remove the confining material that had protected the expensive outfit she was going to wear on her dinner date. Under the vinyl barrier, the teal blue material of the dress clung to the long curves of her body, neither disguising its femininity nor distorting the lines.

At first, Lorelei had been tempted to add deforming padding. But she finally decided that Susan's expertise, the hornrimmed glasses, and her long hair confined in a tight bun, would suit her purpose better when contrasted with the body that even Howard had praised.

As Susan folded the cape away into her large make-up satchel, Lorelei looked into the hand mirror she had used periodically to check her sister's progress and examined the completed job.

Susan had majored in drama and stage production in college. Now that her youngest child was in school, she gave advice about cosmetics to women in their homes, augmenting the family income with product sales. And once a week, the former acting teacher also helped the inmates of the local women's prison produce plays. Her lessons on how to perform and how to use stage make-up subtly countered the lack of self-confidence that affected many of those ladies.

All of her sister's talents were evident in the reflection Lorelei saw in the mirror. Complying with Lorelei's orders, Susan—using very few cosmetics—had transformed her sister into one of the homeliest women in San Diego. And amazingly, even at this close range, Lorelei thought that her face looked very natural . . . naturally plain, that was.

The make-up Susan had lightly brushed on had subtly dulled the normal, healthy glow of Lorelei's skin. Now her fine bone structure was blunted, so that all the interesting angles and curves of Lorelei's face appeared flat and boring. Even her wide mouth looked thin and uninviting.

Lorelei perversely stuck her tongue out at the image, and squinted her blue eyes, whose vibrant color was somehow dimmed by the pale lashes and brows that framed them.

"I agree, I've done the impossible. You are definitely several levels below plain." Susan waved her hands in exasperation. She paced up and down in front of Lorelei, passionately lecturing her.

"Lori, I just don't understand why you want to go out looking like this. Are you punishing yourself because Howard lied and cheated? Don't you realize that *you* didn't do anything wrong? The man is genetically unable to think about anyone but himself. He's a pathological user who trades on his boyish good looks to con everyone he meets. It was just your bad luck that you met him when you were at your most vulnerable to his brand of charm. Why, I'll bet that you never even noticed another male after Howard moved next door when you were fourteen. I mean, until you saw this model fellow.''

Lorelei couldn't prevent her eyes from acknowledging the truth of that statement.

''But, honey,'' Susan pleaded, ''if that's the case, and this man's picture made such an impact on you, why in the world . . .''

Lorelei gritted her teeth and tried to explain just what Daniel Logan and his agent had done. ''Oh, Susan, you should have heard him. He said I was a *matzopunim!*''

''*Matzopunim?*''

''Yeah, that's Yiddish for being as ugly as a piece of matzo, you know, that unleavened bread with all sorts of brown bumps and lines on it.'' Lorelei groaned.

''I know what matzo is. Who said that? Howard? When did he call you? Why do you listen to that two-faced . . .''

''No, not Howard, I haven't spoken to him in months. It was Sherman Schreiber, the model's agent. That's what he told Daniel Logan I looked like when he came to see me. I really was a mess, soaked by that damned sprinkler system and covered with manure. I can understand Schreiber being put off, but he went too far. He had the gaul to make a long-distance call to Logan from my office. I overheard them going into hysterics about my looks.''

''Oh, Lori, you know . . .'' Susan began.

''I know, I know, eavesdroppers never hear anything good about themselves,'' Lorelei interrupted. ''But this time, I'm glad I listened. Wait till tonight! Wait until Daniel Logan takes me to the Hotel Ramona. He'll have to sit there all evening and stare at this wallflower face.

And of course, all those elegant people will be snickering at him. Just think what that will do for his manly ego."

Lorelei finally stopped for a breath, giving her sister a chance to get a word into the conversation.

"Ah ha, this is for revenge! Well, why didn't you say so before? Go get 'em, kid!" Susan urged. Her expression of full support lasted for at least three seconds, before a worried frown again crossed her pretty face. "But what if you see someone you know, honey? Doesn't Mark Tolliver go there a lot, and . . ."

"Mark's still in the mountains," Lorelei broke in. "So I'm not worried about him. And do you really think anyone else is going to recognize me like this?"

"Not likely. Well, maybe this will work out for the best. You've been rooted to this place like one of your potted plants since the divorce. And even if it's just as a joke, at least your juices are stirred up and you're asserting yourself. I've really been worried that you'd developed a martyr complex during all those years you financed Howard's studies. You know that you haven't accepted a single date since your separation and divorce. And not through lack of opportunity. I've heard Mark ask you out half a dozen times, and then there's that editor at the weekly newspaper and . . ."

"Susan, I am *not* a martyr!" Lorelei broke in forcefully. "I know I made a terrible mistake when I supported Howard and didn't finish my own schooling. But I'm working hard to change that. I didn't want to say anything until it came through, but I applied to the University of California at San Diego for the fall semester. I got my acceptance today, and they're even going to give me credit for work experience toward a degree in ornamental horticulture."

"That's great news! Mom and Dad will be thrilled. Heck, I'm thrilled," Susan cheered. "A great beginning.

Now, about getting a new man in your life, too . . . As I said, Mark . . .''

"Oh, Mark is only asking me out as a friend, and the others . . . God, Susan, how can I take a chance on trusting myself with another man? Like you said, I walked around in a daze for years, thinking that Howard and I were the love story of the century. Oh, I wasn't entirely blind. I knew he had his faults. He was very immature about fulfilling any obligation not tied to his medical studies, and his impulsive buying habits wrecked my monthly budget more than once. But I always thought that he loved me, up until the morning I came home unexpectedly and heard him talking to Carol on the phone."

Lorelei fought for control. She would not cry over the weasel.

"No, honey, don't feel like that. Howard is a genius at fooling people. He's the perfect marketing personality; you see only what he wants you to see. That self-serving, conniving, egotistical . . .''

In the middle of Susan's heated denouncement of her former brother-in-law, the door to the kitchen banged open, and Lorelei's sixteen-year-old nephew walked in. Clint wove around lush tropical plants and ducked under the flower-filled hanging pots that were the sum total of Lorelei's decorating efforts.

"Feed me, I'm starving," he announced dramatically, wiping dirt-stained hands over his tattered La Jolla High T-shirt. "I ate lunch at least four hours ago, and Tom made me help him transplant all those kapok trees while I was waiting for you to get done, and . . . Hey, Aunt Lori, what happened to you? I thought Mom said you had a hot date tonight."

Clint's eyes narrowed, examining the results of his mother's artistic talent on his aunt's face.

"Never mind," Susan advised her son. "Just get something from the refrigerator and go wait for me in that rubble-heap you call a car, young man. Of all times for my muffler to fall off, Lori. I even had to cancel my trip to the prison this morning. Thank goodness Clint and his death-mobile got back from the beach early. You were so worked up on the phone, you actually threatened to over-water my begonias when I wasn't sure if I could make it here. As it is," she checked the kitchen clock, "we've finished just in time."

"Hey, Mom, that's a classic Mustang convertible you're putting down."

"Yes, dear, I know, and I really do appreciate the trans-portation," Susan relented. She gave her son the biggest bear hug that a five-foot-zero parent could bestow upon a six-foot-plus child. "OK, now go wait in the car, or Mother will break your kneecaps. Lori and I are dealing with top-secret stuff here, and I don't want the whole town in on it."

"Aw, Mom, I won't breathe a word."

"Out!" The no-nonsense command had the young man moving from the room before he even knew what his size-twelve feet were doing. But taking no chances, Susan locked the door behind her son's retreating back.

Whirling on her sister, Susan used the same uncompro-mising tone on Lorelei. "Now get that picture of Daniel Logan, like you promised. I want to see what he looks like, and then I'll get me and my son out of here before the guy shows up in the flesh."

Without saying a word, Lorelei went to the shelf that held her cookbooks, and retrieved the Sunday supplement magazine containing several good recipes, as well as the picture of Daniel Logan. It automatically fell open to the well-thumbed page when Lorelei handed the booklet to her sister.

Lorelei watched Susan collapse onto a chair, turning the

full-color ad to various angles so that she wouldn't miss the slightest detail of the photograph.

"Wow-ee! And what beautiful flesh he has! What a smile . . . what courage! I can see now why you wrote that letter."

"Oh, Suzie, I can't believe that I wrote a *fan* letter. I'm twenty-seven, for heaven's sake, and I feel like the world's oldest groupie!" Lorelei groaned.

"Honey, don't worry about it; this is a guy who would have made a teenybopper out of Queen Victoria! And after seeing the ad, I feel the urge to get out some stationery, myself. I've written a few fan letters in my day. Did I ever tell you how Clint got his name?"

Susan's mischievous giggle joined her sister's laughter. But then a sudden speculative gleam lit Susan's eyes.

"Hey, Lori, now that I think of it, all I ever got for my efforts was an autographed picture. That must have been one hell of a unique letter you wrote to generate this kind of a response from Logan's agent. And that means this guy with the overgrown kitty-cat on his shoulders *really* threw you for a loop. Too bad he turned out to be such a jerk."

Both women started abruptly at the sound of a fist pounding on the apartment door. The barrage was followed by a muffled voice. "Aunt Lori, open up, your date's here," Clint announced through the locked partition.

"Oh, God, he's here," Lorelei whispered to her sister in sudden terror. The insane position she had put herself into finally registered in her brain. "Susan, you answer the door. Send him away. Tell him that I've got the flu . . . bubonic plague . . . leprosy!"

"Now, just pull yourself together, Lorelei Hunt. Are you going to let this man get away with the names he's called you? Are you going to allow another male to trample all over you? You've got more pride than that! Go get your purse, while I let him in.'' Susan pushed her taller sibling out of the room.

In her bedroom, Lorelei staggered over to the dresser. Feeling on the edge of panic, she took several deep breaths to control her shaking hands. When they steadied, Lorelei picked up her clutch, automatically stuffing keys, identification, and make-up into it.

A mumble of conversation in the other room suddenly became clearer as the people outside moved closer to her slightly opened door.

''Of course, you can call me Dan, Susan. You know, I can't believe that you're actually Clint's mother. Did your husband have to serve much time for taking a child bride?'' A deep, husky laugh that must belong to Daniel Logan was joined by the familiar sound of Susan's giggle.

''Heavens, Dan, my husband, John, and I were more than old enough when we married. And I know you're too much of a gentleman to ask, but Lorelei is my younger sister, more than twelve years younger.'' Susan purred in a voice that contained none of the sisterly chauvinism of a few minutes ago.

''Ah, Dan, I'd love to continue this wonderful chat, but I know you two have to get going. I just popped in to help Lorelei with a . . . a . . . project. And all of a sudden, I think I'd better change some of the details before she leaves. Clint, go out to the potting shed to see if Tom needs any more help.''

After a few seconds of mumbled protest from her nephew, Lorelei heard the sound of her kitchen door closing.

''Dan, why don't you sit down and make yourself comfortable?'' Susan said. ''Lori is going to be a minute or two.''

From her position on the other side of the door, Lorelei

fumed. The thought that her own sister had gone over to the enemy camp had an immediate effect on her backbone, spreading rigid strength along its length. Jamming her horn-rimmed glasses on her nose, she was suddenly determined to play out the charade she had concocted to its ultimate, embarrassing end. Embarrassing for Daniel Logan, she vowed.

Throwing the door wide, she rushed forward, only to collide with Susan. Their hands automatically went out to each other, as they tried to counter the force of the impact. Lorelei staggered, and bending from the waist, she gripped her tiny sister's shoulders to keep the smaller woman from crashing to the floor. In the process, much of Lorelei's thick, long hair shook out of its confining bun and fell forward, covering her face completely.

"You're making a terrible mistake," Susan hissed into Lorelei's ear. "Let's go cream this make-up off before he sees you," she whispered, frantically tugging at her sister.

But it was too late. Daniel Logan had already risen, and through the screen of her hair, Lorelei saw feet clad in dress loafers approach her and Susan. As she looked higher, she noticed long-fingered, masculine hands reaching out to help them regain their balance.

Sherman Schreiber must have gone round the bend, Daniel thought as he moved across the room. Or maybe his agent had taken up secret drinking, he decided as his eyes slowly assessed Lorelei Hunt, or at least her hair and body.

Even during the last three years of modeling, Daniel had never seen a woman with such a magnificent pale blond mane. Unable to make out her facial features through the thick cascade of hair, his gaze automatically traveled down to her body.

It was evident that she was tall and slender, and that her dress clung lovingly to a perfectly proportioned form.

Daniel knew that his mouth had fallen open in surprise. But he couldn't seem to control his jaw muscles. He also couldn't prevent the instant reaction in another part of his body when he noticed the long length of leg Lorelei Hunt revealed from a thigh-high slit in her skirt.

Why in the world had Sherman called this lady a dog? Daniel wondered, as the woman found her balance and stood away from her smaller sister.

Lorelei straightened to her full height and threw back her head to get the hair out of her face. The defiant gesture resettled the mass into a gilded frame that pulled Daniel Logan's attention away from her body and focused his eyes on her features for the first time.

Waves of shock bounced back and forth between the two of them, but not for the same reasons.

While Daniel finally understood what Sherman Schreiber meant by a *matzopunim*, Lorelei almost staggered under the tremendous impact of the model's beauty.

She had examined his picture a hundred times, but now she *saw* him for the first time. His features were strong, chiseled, uncompromising. Nose, cheekbones, and chin were all molded to form the most compelling face she had ever seen. Such purity of line would have been cold, almost graven, if Daniel Logan's skin and hair had been tinted differently. But a bronzed glow subtly softened the sharp cast of his bones, and burnished auburn hair fell in an appealing lock over a wide forehead.

Unexpectedly, Lorelei saw that a spattering of freckles dusted the straight bridge of his nose and the high slant of his cheekbones. This man would cause the most delightful dilemma for a woman. Her first reaction would be to drape herself pliantly over his six-foot, four-inch body in abject submission to his every desire. But then she'd be tempted to brush wayward red hair off that broad forehead, and rest his freckled cheek against the maternal expanse of her breast.

Lorelei never determined just how long she and Daniel Logan were locked in their first flesh-to-flesh glimpse of each other. But finally, the meaning of the stunned look in his eyes penetrated to Lorelei's brain, and her renewed anger with the man melted the frozen tableau they had shared.

As Lorelei moved an abrupt step backward, Daniel tore his gaze away from her to stare at Susan's pixy features and petite form in total disbelief.

"You can't be sisters!" he challenged. He dared one or the other of the pair to refute the observations his eyes had made. One woman was tiny and wholesomely pretty, the other was tall and . . . *homely*. There was no kinder word Daniel could think of to describe Lorelei Hunt, who glared up at him, clearly aware of the contrasting picture she and her sister presented.

"Oh, we are sisters . . . truly," Susan breathed. "Of course, I take after Mom, while Dad and Lorelei won a look-alike contest when she was in grade school."

"The poor kid," Daniel whispered.

"What did you say?" Lorelei finally opened her mouth with that demand, pushing her wayward hair back into its bun.

"I . . . oh, nothing important." He desperately struggled to control his expression and his wayward tongue, not wanting to say anything else that might hurt this unfortunate woman. Imagining the comments she must have endured over the years, when compared to her sister, Daniel suddenly vowed to make this evening a happy event for Lorelei Hunt.

As the model's attention traveled from Susan to her again, Lorelei watched the shock drain out of his eyes, to be replaced with an amalgam of expressions, none of which made her feel very good. Just maybe she had made a terrible mistake in judging his character, she thought, looking at the play of emotions in his eyes.

Compassion, pity, and regret, all moved in devastating order across his expressive irises, as his gaze went from Lorelei's face to her body and back to her face again. Those feelings were finally replaced by resignation, as the tall man straightened the sleeve of his well-cut dinner jacket. With courtly kindness, he then offered his impressively muscled arm to Lorelei.

"We really should get going, Ms. Hunt. We don't want to miss our reservations."

"Well, you two have a good time," Susan admonished, recovering her normal voice. "Have you ever been to the Hotel Ramona before, Dan?"

"No, and I'm looking forward to it. I've heard it's architecture is unique in this area, a real turn-of-the-century treasure."

"It is that," Susan agreed. "But sort of hidden away, and unusual. Disguised from the real world, one might say. But that's true of so many things, isn't it, Daniel? It's amazing what jewels you can find under the most unlikely surfaces. One should always remember that, don't you think?"

Lorelei gave her sister a grimace, which didn't add to her worldly beauty one bit. She got Daniel Logan out of the room before Susan began spouting clichés about books and their covers or diamonds in the rough.

A molded fiberglass marvel of the automotive age waited for them on Lorelei's driveway. Sliding into the Corvette's richly upholstered seat, she sniffed the elegant leather aroma as Daniel got in and carefully closed the door on his side of the midnight blue car.

"Mmmm, smells lovely, and about two hours old," she

commented, while he coaxed a powerful purr out of the responsive engine.

"Three months," he corrected, "and I still live in fear that the stable of horses under the hood will run away with me."

"Why would you spend a fortune for a car you weren't sure you could handle?" Lorelei scoffed.

"I didn't buy it. Sherm Schreiber leases it, as a tax deduction."

"Tax deduction?" Lorelei really laughed for the first time in hours. "Tax deduction!"

"Yeah, it's part of my image." Daniel chuckled as if he also found himself a genuine source of entertainment.

"Well, that's reasonable, you being the 'fastest-rising male model in the country,' and all," Lorelei teased. "I wonder what excuse Howard came up with to justify his new Maserati to the IRS."

"Howard?"

"Dr. Howard Taylor, M.D.; P.C.; and S.O.B. My ex-husband. I took back my maiden name when we were divorced," Lorelei revealed. She hadn't wanted to keep anything that tied her to Howard. Not a stick of furniture from the apartment they had shared . . . not a penny of alimony.

"*You* were married?" Daniel blurted, before he could censor his tongue.

As the model's eyes scanned the face Susan had designed, Lorelei nodded. "For eight years," she confirmed coolly. And any thought she might have had about quickly ending this farce vanished with his incredulous stare.

It seemed that she hadn't misjudged him, after all, Lorelei realized. God, the man was shallow; he was only concerned with appearances. Even with Susan's handiwork, Lorelei knew that she didn't look monstrous . . . just very plain. But it was obvious that Daniel was so narrow-minded that he had nothing to do with women who weren't perfect. And she suddenly wondered just what Sherman Schreiber had to promise Daniel in return for taking her out this evening. Clothing? A motorcycle? Maybe a yacht.

The thought of him taking a bribe goaded her into icily quoting a statistic she remembered. "Most of us do marry, you know. Almost ninety-six percent of the female population will be married sometime during their lives."

"Oh, I realize that," he hastened to assure her. And trying to make up for his gaffe, Daniel rushed on without thinking.

"And you said your marriage lasted for eight years. That's forever these days. Why did he divorce you after all that time?" God, where was his self-control, Daniel silently groaned. "Hey, I'm sorry, Ms. Hunt, I don't know what's happened to my manners. That question was entirely out of line."

"Oh, please do call me Lori, Daniel. And I don't mind answering your questions about Howard, I'm quite over the man. Carol is welcome to him," she avowed. "Carol's the other woman, of course."

"The other woman . . . I see. Well, I'll bet it was a case of 'mid-life crisis.' He probably wanted to prove he wasn't getting older by marrying a . . . ah, someone younger."

Daniel was trying so valiantly to keep from putting his over-sized foot into his gorgeous mouth again that Lorelei almost had to feel sorry for him. Almost.

"Actually, I think sweet Carol is a bit older than I am. And in all honesty, nobody would say that she's better looking . . . if *that* thought might have crossed your mind," Lorelei assured him with utmost sincerity.

"Then why in the world did he do it?" Daniel knew he should just shut up, but for some strange reason, he felt angry at the man who had left Lorelei and seemed unable to leave the subject of Howard Taylor's defection.

"Oh, it's really very simple," Lorelei patiently explained. "You see, Carol's souffles never fall."

Somehow, she managed to carry off the quip and put a lilt of laughter into her voice. But Lorelei abruptly turned away from Daniel, to stare blindly at the passing landscape.

_____ THREE _____

Like everything else that evening, the drive to the hotel didn't go as Lorelei had planned. Daniel Logan wouldn't let her continue the hostile silence she tried to maintain after explaining about Howard.

Saying that he had never been in the city before, Daniel had dozens of questions about the area. And very reluctantly, Lorelei found herself relating the history of this building and the significance of that landmark.

Daniel seemed especially interested in the "Blue Bridge," as residents affectionately called the curving engineer's dream that linked San Diego and their destination, the town of Coronado.

During her childhood Lorelei had lived in the small city, just a few miles from the Hotel Ramona. But somehow she had never visited the place. When they finally reached the western shore of Coronado and pulled into the hotel's parking lot, she gasped at her first close-up look at the building.

Looming high and wide on the edge of a dramatic sea cliff, the sixteen-gabled mansion flew huge flags that snapped smartly in the constant ocean breeze. And it seemed to Lorelei that the vivid green-and-white structure's hundreds of mullioned windows smiled at her in warm welcome.

Daniel was also entranced with the building. He remained suspended for several seconds, half-in and half-out of his door, staring at the incredible construction. *God, what I wouldn't give to have lived when these kinds of buildings were being designed*, he thought.

Forcefully shaking himself out of his daze, he finally moved around the car to help Lorelei from the low-slung machine.

Well-placed lighting guided the pair as they walked along the paths that curved around the building. Unusual flowering shrubs and beds of annuals decorated the way. Hardly realizing what she was doing, Lorelei began an enthusiastic monologue, giving Daniel a professional's evaluation of the beautifully landscaped grounds.

Caught up in her discourse, Lorelei automatically bent down to pull out a stray dandelion that must have escaped the notice of the grounds crew.

"No pity for a poor plant that's just trying to move into a better neighborhood?" Daniel joked.

As Lorelei laughed up at Daniel, her masquerading features caught the full illumination of the nearest street light. She almost cried out in fury when she saw the grin on Daniel's face wobble, and that now familiar look of pity enter his eyes.

Once again, Lorelei's incredible plainness made Daniel want to take this poor brave woman into his arms. Though she had shrugged off eight years of marriage with a little joke, when they talked in the car, Daniel had seen the hint of tears that glistened in her eyes while she talked of her ex-husband's betrayal.

He wanted to say something that would ease a little of

her pain, but before he could think of anything, Lorelei abruptly turned and hurried down the path toward the hotel.

"Hey, wait for me," he called after her. It took Daniel several long strides to catch up. He reached Lorelei's side just in time to take her elbow before she started up the wide, marble stairway that led to the outside entrance of the hotel's dining room.

At the touch of Daniel's hand on her arm, Lorelei tried to pull away from him, only to feel a moment of nightmarish panic when a small, but noisy, riot suddenly formed around them.

Completely disoriented, she would have fallen off the step if Daniel's firm hand hadn't supported her. It was only after the raucous crowd pushed past them that Lorelei realized the people were pursuing a small, voluptuous woman and a slim, tuxedo-clad man, who had just been escorted out of a stretch limousine by a broad-chested wall of bodyguards. The impressive couple, and their human shield, ploughed relentlessly through the milling crowd, which somehow encircled Lorelei and Daniel again.

There was a blinding light, and a swarm of photographers surged forward, almost knocking Lorelei off her feet.

"For God's sake, don't shove this lady," Daniel shouted.

Sheltering Lorelei, he straight-armed the nearest offenders. His wide shoulders cleared a path through the straining press as he maneuvered them up the steps.

"Come on, Miss Crowley, Mr. Trainor, give us a smile. It's only two days into your honeymoon. You must have enough energy left to smile, don't you?" The cheeky comment from one of the reporters generated good-natured guffaws from the crowd.

Lorelei saw the couple turn, and she belatedly recog-

nized them as the well-publicized leads in a popular evening soap. The pair threw back their heads in shared
amusement. Glamorous shoulders shrugged simultane-
ously, and the two smiled down at the heckler.

"OK! Now, how about a kiss?" the persistent man
goaded.

They ardently complied with the challenge, as dozens
of powerful flashes outlined the couple in intimate detail.

"Say, who's the other guy up there? He's a hunk."
Feminine tones pierced the general hubbub. "But get a
load of the dame he's with!"

Both Lorelei and Daniel automatically turned to find the
source of the rude comment in the crowd. And yet another
round of light flared, aimed right into their faces. Caught
by surprise, Lorelei and Daniel peered out at the mass of
humanity, mouths slightly opened.

"Must be some gigolo out with his sugarmomma." At
the snickered reply Lorelei's complexion turned from delicate pink to fiery red.

Uttering a stinging expletive, Daniel made a sudden end
run around the engrossed television personalities. He
pulled Lorelei up the remaining steps and into the gloom
of the restaurant's entry hall.

Blinking furiously to regain her vision and composure,
Lorelei leaned against the heavy brocade curtain that hung
around the entry door. A warm hand on her shoulder
squeezed gently.

"I think I may have to order a Seeing Eye dog," Daniel
complained. "Being rich and famous does have its draw-
backs, doesn't it?" His husky laughter was warm in her
ear.

"Remind me to refuse all future television offers,
Dan."

Lorelei smiled up at the blur that had to be Daniel's
face. And in that instant, her eyes adjusted to the gloom,

focusing just in time to see a wry grimace disappearing from his expressive set of features. But his thoughts had already been clearly telegraphed to her: Lorelei Hunt never would have to worry about star status . . . not with that face . . . not in this life.

Any gratitude she might have felt because of Daniel's protectiveness on the steps of the hotel vanished. Lord, she was getting sick and tired of trying to figure out if this man was a hero or a jerk. She had changed her mind about him half a dozen times since he walked into her apartment an hour ago.

Well, as of this minute, Lorelei had no doubt that he fit into the jerk category. And knowing that she was about to ruin her exquisitely planned revenge by telling him so, she mumbled an incoherent excuse and rushed off to find the ladies' lounge.

A minute later, she stood next to an elegant marble sink, shaking with rage. Lorelei savagely twisted the antique brass fitting to run a fierce stream of cold water into the bowl. She longed to splash her burning cheeks with the liquid. But even though Susan had assured her that the make-up needed to be creamed off, Lorelei didn't want to chance blurring her sister's masterpiece. She was not about to rid herself of the disguise until it had served its purpose.

That man needed to be taken down several pegs. He needed to know what it was like to be snickered at . . . to be whispered about . . . to be cast aside when you're no longer useful.

She'd show Howard just what it felt like to . . . Howard? No, Daniel . . . Daniel Logan! Shaking her head to clear it, Lorelei let the chilling stream run over her wrists, and slowly felt her face cool and her blood pressure fall.

When she was in complete control again, she dried off her hands and walked back into the reception area. Daniel stood where Lorelei had left him, just inside the lead-glassed entry door. But he was not alone. He was talking intently to a short young man with a crew cut. As Lorelei walked slowly toward the pair, the small man reached up to hit Daniel on the shoulder with a hard, comradely clap, then turned and disappeared into the night. The door closed on the young man just as Lorelei came up behind Daniel.

"Is our table ready?" she asked calmly.

Daniel whirled around. "Oh . . . you're back already!" He felt a surge of red sweep over his cheekbones. He rapidly went over the conversation with Todd Jenkins in his mind, trying to remember just what he had said to him. Pretty bland stuff, he thought, although you never could be sure with those people. . . .

"I asked if our table is ready," Lorelei repeated.

The edge in her voice penetrated Daniel's thoughts. "Ah . . . I was just going to check, when . . ."

"When you met a friend," she finished for him.

"No, just an acquaintance, from Los Angeles. Small world, isn't it?" Daniel tossed off tritely. His eyes danced over her face. What had he said about Lorelei? Had he explained himself correctly . . . ?

"Daniel?" Lorelei prompted when she saw his attention focus inwardly again.

Shaking his head, Daniel took a deep breath. What did it matter just how he had phrased it? *He* knew what he had meant.

"Well, what are we waiting for? Let's see about our table," he said heartily. Taking Lorelei's elbow, he guided her over to the entrance of the dining room.

As they stopped at the threshold, the hostess looked up from her lists and smiled impersonally at the pair. Lorelei barely kept from snickering as the woman's lashes started fluttering when she got a good look at Daniel Logan.

"Good evening, sir!" she purred seductively. "Under what name was your reser-va . . . vation?"

The woman's manners were impeccable; Lorelei had to give her that. Only her slight stutter revealed the astonishment she must have felt when she glanced over to check out the female who could attract such a beautiful man.

However, that little lapse made Lorelei's day. Oh, how Daniel was going to hate being here with her! The next couple of hours were going to be hell for someone as superficial as he was.

Lorelei cheered silently as she heard the hostess assure Daniel that she was giving him one of the best tables . . . center dining room, with an ocean view. The smitten woman didn't seem to understand his urgent request for a more intimate location.

And with a timing that Lorelei couldn't have improved upon, the *maître d'* arrived to lead the mismatched couple arrogantly through the nautically decorated room before Daniel could say another word.

At first she had to struggle to keep from grinning. However, that hint of a smile quickly disappeared when their passage across the aqua-tinted grotto provoked a tempest that blew Lorelei right off her revenge-fueled course.

She watched the same scenario play out at every table they passed. The occupants glanced up with casual human curiosity as they neared. Then years of social training flew out the window when each and every individual did a classic double-take.

Lorelei knew that the contrast between her washed-out features and Daniel's handsome face was just too much for the patrons. She listened as table after table erupted into nervous tittering and malicious speculation.

One particularly loud exchange seemed to sum up everyone's thoughts.

"Oh, the poor thing!" a woman stage-whispered nearby.

"Who are you talking about, her or him?" her male companion countered.

A second after Lorelei heard that bit of witty dialogue, Daniel's firm arm suddenly embraced her shoulders and stopped her progress through the gauntlet she walked.

He turned her and cupped her face with strong, long-fingered hands. Forced to look up at him, Lorelei's cry of surprise seemed very loud in the abruptly silent room.

Lorelei's eyes widened as she felt the green-gold flame of Daniel's gaze flicker over her pale cheeks and flare against the altered lines of her mouth.

He really hates me for dragging him here, she thought wildly. *And now he's going to denounce me and leave me all alone to face this sadistic crowd.*

Daniel *was* in a fury. He wanted to kick over tables and punch the spiteful mouths that had put this look of suffering into Lorelei's homely, sweet face. Then a sudden inspiration struck him, and with a slight lift of his upper lip, a snarl of rage changed into a wry grin.

"Let's really give them something to talk about," he said thickly.

And to Lorelei's surprise, he reached out to remove and pocket her glasses. As his incredibly beautiful mouth lowered toward hers, Lorelei finally understood that his anger had been directed at the spectators, not at her.

The kiss didn't last long, just long enough for Lorelei's lips to part, and for Daniel's tongue to stroke hers in a fiery salute. Feeling as if her bones were dissolving, she sagged in his arms. As her body pressed limply against his, Daniel pulled his mouth off her lips. He instantly put an arm around her shoulders, and with a signal to the waiting *maître d'*, Daniel supported her the rest of the way to their table.

Lorelei was so bedazzled by the force of Daniel's kiss that she didn't see the long, surprised stare he gave her as he carefully placed her overheated body on the overstuffed chair.

What in the hell is happening here, Daniel asked himself as he tugged at the collar of his shirt. This was crazy! Oh, he liked Lorelei—he appreciated her knowledge of plants—he admired her ability to joke about her husband's defection, even though the man obviously had hurt her badly. But how could he have responded *physically* to a woman who looked like Lorelei Hunt?

It was true that he hadn't been with anybody in a long time, but he saw raving beauties every day when he was modeling, and he had never felt such an overwhelming caveman urge to sweep up a lady in his arms and go find the nearest bed. His reaction to Lorelei went against all of his previous experience, all of his principles.

Daniel glanced sharply over to see if she was aware of the discomfort the taste of her mouth and the feel of her body had caused him. But only the top of her shiny head peeked above the oversized menu.

He took a deep drink of iced water, and slowly felt himself regain control of his raging hormones. Seeing the waiter glancing at their table, he forced his attention to the food list.

"Since neither of us has been here before, Lorelei," he called across the table, "why don't we ask the waiter to recommend something?"

When Daniel's deep voice finally penetrated the fog in which her mind wandered, Lorelei lowered her menu.

"Huh?" she said. *That's right, kid, dazzle him with your wit*, she mentally kicked herself. "What a wonderful idea," she managed to get out on her next attempt.

In fact, she thought that Daniel's suggestion was brilliant. Especially since her eyes seemed incapable of focusing well enough to read the finely printed menu. For some reason, everything just beyond the model's imposing form blurred like a dream sequence in a pretentious art film. Her glasses would have helped the situation, but in her muddle, Lorelei completely forgot that the old hornrims rested in Daniel's breast pocket.

Soliciting the waiter's help, Daniel didn't pretend to be an expert as they discussed the food and wine. The man seemed genuinely pleased to have his opinions asked for, and he assured the couple that they would have a meal that neither would forget.

How true, how true, Lorelei groaned to herself. She had set out to embarrass Daniel Logan, sure that he was a shallow, insensitive hunk. Well, he had just proved that he deserved to be on the hero's list, and all she had accomplished was to make a total fool of herself. Sinking deeper into her chair, Lorelei struggled to find some way out of the mess she had created . . . anything that wouldn't completely ruin this evening.

The depths of her remorse became more and more profound as Daniel kept the conversation going. While she pushed her salad around the plate, he gently teased at the pall of depression that enfolded her.

"I wonder if Mumford ever visited this place," he said, as his glance took in the rich, intricate detailing that characterized the Victorian style.

"Mumford?" Lorelei asked, finally raising her head.

"Louis Mumford," he clarified.

But not enough for the woman seated across from him. Lorelei continued to look puzzled.

"Among other things, he wrote *The Brown Decades,* a history of the architecture of the 1880s," Daniel continued. "That was the height of Victorian influence on buildings constructed all over the world. And I think this hotel, this room, would have pleased him. It's taken the best ideas from that time and blended them with the raw American enthusiasm of the day. Look around you, Lori . . .

feel the strength . . . smell the elegance. Luxury and usefulness blend perfectly here. This is a structure that will have significance for as long as it stands. It was built of its age, but it was also created for the ages. . . ."

Daniel stopped abruptly, the flush tinting his high cheekbones momentarily masking the spattering of freckles on them. He opened his mouth to apologize for delivering a lecture, but Lorelei interrupted him before the first word could leave his lips.

"Oh, Daniel! What a marvelous insight," she cried, forgetting her dilemma for the moment. "I've never looked at a building like that . . . as an expression of the age in which it was built, but I'll certainly try to from now on. Have you always been so aware of architectural history?" she asked.

Surprise flitted across Daniel's face. He never had met a woman outside of the Architecture Department who appreciated his enthusiasm about the past. Grinning broadly, he answered her question.

"Not really, I only found out how fascinating it was a few years ago. But now it's become a compulsion. I've been reading everything I can get my hands on. I guess it's the same with you and plants. You gave me quite a course in commercial landscaping on our way in from the parking lot."

"Well, I was impressed," she countered. "Do you know how much work goes into planning landscaping on such a scale?"

"I'm not complaining, Lori. I admire the depth of your knowledge," Daniel said quickly. "I didn't get much of a chance to look around your nursery, but what I saw while Clint led me through your showroom was extraordinary. How long have you owned the business?"

"About six months. I inherited it when my grandfather died. But I worked with him most of my life. He left the nursery to me just after my legal separation, so Howard didn't get to claim it as community property," she muttered bitterly.

"Sounds like it's been a rough year for you," Daniel said softly.

"Yes," Lorelei agreed absently, her thoughts turning inward. The last six months had been filled with upheaval, illness, and loss. She still had to guard against the depression her grandfather's death, her mother's heart problems, and Howard's defection had caused her.

But that sour thought was immediately diluted by memories of her grandfather's loving gift, which had neutralized much of the acid of her divorce. And taking a deep breath, Lorelei found herself telling Daniel about her mother's father—Gunnar Swensen—who, even in death, had given purpose to her life.

"In his will, Granddad said that the nursery was my genetic inheritance, the occupation I was born to. He had very strange ideas about education and society. He thought everyone had a job they naturally fitted into, no formal training required . . ."

Daniel almost gasped when he saw the sparkle in Lorelei's eyes. As she spoke, her enthusiasm for her subject seemed to overcome the paleness of her lashes and eyebrows. She managed to look beautiful, somehow.

Lorelei stopped talking abruptly when she noticed the expression on Daniel's face. He watched her with a strange intensity. But before she could comment, Daniel visibly shook himself and urged her to continue.

"He sounds like an original," he prompted.

"Oh, he was that," she agreed with a little laugh.

And his theories had suited Howard just fine, Lorelei remembered. In fact, her ex-husband had squashed her attempts to complete a formal degree in ornamental horticulture. She wanted to go to college at night, because he was often in the hospital forty-eight hours at a time. But Howard had been afraid that Lorelei wouldn't be able to put in her normal long hours at work, and that her grandfather would dock her pay. The money had provided essentials at first, and then the luxuries that Howard seemed to need, more and more.

Suddenly aware that Daniel sat waiting to hear the rest of her explanation, Lorelei mentally backtracked to her last sentence.

"Maybe Granddad was right. I probably learned all I'll ever need to run the business while at his knee. In fact, I can't recall a time when I wasn't up to my elbows in manu . . . excuse me, in organic fertilizer. And he didn't even have to train me; it was already in my genes."

Lorelei gave Daniel a mock glare of outrage when he broke into husky chuckles at the image she had drawn.

"Oh, I'd say it was environment, more than genetics, Lori."

"Not in my family. Everything is in our genes, and I can prove it. Now, don't tell my sister that I told you this," Lorelei leaned across the table, lowering her voice to a conspirator's whisper, "but Susan used to suck her fingers. Not her thumb, the last two fingers on her right hand. I wasn't around at the time, but my mother told me all about it, and we have a couple of baby pictures with Suzie sucking away."

"Lori, please don't tell me that she still . . ."

"Oh, no. She's over the habit, thank God. I don't think it lasted much past her sixth or seventh birthday. But the point of this story is that her daughter, Amelia, does the same thing, but Clint never did. Genetic, right? Now, don't tell me that you haven't seen something similar in your own family tree."

"I wouldn't know. I don't have any ancestors to hang on a tree," he murmured.

"No ancestors, but of course you have to have . . . oh," Lorelei faltered.

"Yeah," Daniel confirmed, "your classic case of the unclaimed baby found in a trashcan."

"Oh . . ." was all Lorelei could think to say. But then she mentally kicked herself for her inelegant handling of the situation. Trying to make up for her clumsiness, she said, "Well then, what about your adoptive family? They must have some inborn traits."

"I was never adopted, Lorelei."

"Daniel!" She placed a comforting hand on his arm, trying to apologize tactilely for the painful memories she must have dredged up. "Daniel, why weren't you adopted? I thought that there were always hundreds of potential parents waiting for each healthy infant."

"Ah . . . healthy. That was the operative word, Lorelei. You see, my hours in the trash didn't do me a lot of good. It might have been the cold of a St. Louis spring night. Or perhaps it was because of the bacteria that shared my temporary garbage can home, but I got sick an awful lot until I was seven or eight. I must have had a hundred colds, and pneumonia at least three times."

Daniel paused in his bitter story, a tale that Lorelei was sure he had never shared before. As he looked at her disguised features, she knew that he imagined her plain face had caused *her* years of agony. And Lorelei fleetingly was glad about how she looked tonight. Daniel Logan never would have let her know of his own pain if he wasn't certain that she was a fellow sufferer.

He drew a deep breath, and then went on, examining his long fingers as he talked. "No, I was not your chubby-cheeked, gurgling baby. There wasn't anybody willing to take on such a chronically ill child. And by the time I outgrew my susceptibility, I was a surly son-of-a-gun. I thought nobody would love me, so I made sure that they couldn't. I constantly got into trouble, not trusting anyone except myself. Oh, they tried to place me, but I must have been sent back a dozen times after trial periods with prospective parents.''

Daniel glanced up at Lorelei. ''Oh, hell, Lori, don't cry!'' He bit off a more potent expletive.

''No, I'm not crying, just a wayward eyelash,'' she protested. Lorelei carefully dabbed the tears off her cheeks, and then found herself reassuring him fiercely. ''Daniel, whoever your ancestors were, I think they gave you wonderful genes. And I'm sure they were strong, handsome, very intelligent people!''

He made a valiant attempt to smile. ''Perhaps you're right, Lori. But I still hated them until I finally realized that I couldn't blame anyone but myself for what happens in my life. About three years ago, at the ripe old age of twenty-five, I finally grew up enough to know that I have to make my own heritage. I looked into myself and decided just what it was that I actually wanted to be. And once I knew, I vowed to do everything necessary to get there.''

The strength of that declaration stunned Lorelei for a second. It suddenly reminded her of Howard's drive to become a plastic surgeon. Yet, she shouldn't have been surprised at Daniel's words. She had sensed his determination to reach some goal, from the first time she had seen him in that infamous ad.

But even if Daniel was driven, did it have to mean that he was a user like Howard? Lorelei asked herself. He hadn't said anything tonight to indicate that he was unscrupulous. But perhaps she had been blinded by his physical beauty, and hadn't seen the real man behind his fantastic façade.

Lorelei shook her head and forced herself to review what he actually *had* said. "So you took stock of your assets and decided to make yourself the best person you could be," she summed up his statements. Nothing wrong with that, she had to admit.

Similar plans had been going through her mind since the demise of her marriage. She was definitely going back to college in the fall. And if she could get her book finished this summer, the large advance George Tolliver had mentioned would take care of any mechanical disaster in the nursery, with enough left over to pay for her tuition.

"Assets, that's it exactly." Daniel broke into her thoughts. "Except, I didn't have much to work with . . . no educational base to fall back on. I messed up any chance I had to go on to college by playing around in high school. After that I worked at a dozen jobs, but experience at waiting tables and washing cars wouldn't take me where I wanted to be.

"So when I happened to read an ad describing the 'Man's World of Modeling,' I asked myself, why not?" He chuckled wryly. "A few, ah . . . people had mentioned the idea to me in the past, and when I finally investigated that prospect, I found out that the money's fantastic. I located a legitimate agent—that's right, Sherman Schreiber—and he trained me to project 'The Look.' The rest is history."

" 'The Look'?" Lorelei echoed in confusion.

But he didn't answer. Daniel abruptly became stock-still. The warm, handsome man Lorelei had been talking with disappeared. And in his place sat a cold, marble-cut statue of human perfection. She couldn't contain the startled gasp that sprang from her throat.

" 'The Look,' " Daniel suddenly announced, as the icy disdain on his face melted back into the vibrant appeal that Lorelei had found so enchanting all evening long.

"You are amazing," she breathed. "I always thought they got that effect with an inch of make-up and ruthless retouching. You did it with just your attitude."

"Damn right! I wouldn't let anyone plaster that gunk on me. Do you know that some of the guys even use lipstick and mascara. I mean real guys, honest-to-goodness, women-loving men, for God's sake!"

An extended fit of giggles erupted from Lorelei as she reacted to Daniel's vehement indignation. "You mean you never wear make-up of any kind?" she finally sputtered.

"Well . . . ah . . . I have to let them cover the freckles," he muttered.

"What did you say?"

"I said, they went to the mat about the freckles."

"Ah, well, that is definitely a mistake. Dan, if you really want to be the 'hottest male model in America,' like dear Mr. Schreiber proclaims, don't let them touch the freckles anymore. Any woman would think that they're marvelous!"

"Well, it was the one time I agreed with the make-up artists. These damned spots have gotten me into a hundred fights. But they're not as bad as they used to be, and I have hopes that, by the time I'm forty, they'll all be gone. Even if they're not, it won't matter by then. I certainly won't be posing with mountain lions at that age!"

He lifted his eyes to the heavens as if in fervent prayer.

"And don't you dare ask me anything about that beast," he suddenly glared.

Lorelei raised defensive palms, eloquently using them to disavow any interest in the animal. Daniel chuckled, and reached across the table, lacing his fingers with Lorelei's more slender ones. He looked at her finely constructed hands, and then abruptly raised probing eyes to examine her face.

Beautiful hands, magnificent hair, a classic profile . . . maybe she'll take some advice, Daniel thought.

Lorelei watched that puzzled crease appear between Daniel's eyebrows again as he made a careful inventory of her features. Expecting an imminent unmasking, she almost groaned in relief at his next words.

"Lori, you'd really never know I had them when they get done . . . my freckles, I mean. Those make-up people can work miracles. You should see some of the models when they walk in. It's hard to believe anyone would pay for their pictures. But by the time the experts are through with them, you'd swear they were always gorgeous. I guess it's a matter of good bone structure and emphasis."

He ran a light finger along the high plane of Lorelei's cheek. The finger stopped suddenly, retraced its route, and then repeated the sequence again.

The make-up wasn't coming off on his finger! Susan's promise that cold cream would be needed to remove the subtle shading was true. Yet, Lorelei found herself wishing that Daniel's gentle touch had unmasked her. She had let this farce go on too long. She should have told him about her ruse when they first sat down at the table. He really was going to hate her now.

But as Daniel stroked her cheek yet again, she found herself unable to speak. She was on the verge of melting, even though she knew that he had nothing sensual in mind with this exploration.

"You know, I just realized what nice cheekbones you have. It's strange, I can't see them, even this close to you. I have to touch them." He sat there for long seconds, looking at her face. He finally took a deep breath and picked up her hand again. "Lori . . . can I be frank with you for a minute?"

When she nodded reluctantly, Daniel continued. "People tend to judge others by their outward appearance. They often don't take time to see past the skin and bones, to inner qualities. Human nature. It's not very nice at times, but that's the way it is. And those who don't conform to the mold society sets for beauty have to pay a terrible price in being taunted, or even just ignored.'' That deep sigh lifted his wide chest again.

Lord, guide my tongue, Daniel thought, sending up a quick little prayer. ''Lori, I think you're one of the nicest, most interesting women I've ever met. But, at the risk of sounding awfully shallow, I don't think I would have noticed you in a crowd, either. And that makes me very angry with myself, because then I'd never have found out just what a lovely person you really are.''

He put up a sudden hand to ward off the heated reply he expected when Lorelei opened her mouth, not realizing that she was going to apologize, to end the stupid masquerade and tell him that *he* was one of the nicest human beings she had ever met.

''Daniel, there's something I have to t-tell you . . .'' Lorelei stuttered.

But Daniel's words cut in over hers. ''Listen to me, honey. You could look a lot better; you're just not fulfilling your own potential. For some reason, you seem to have maximized your bad points, and completely ignored the good ones. I don't understand it, you've got beautiful hair, a wonderful body, and you taste . . . you taste . . .''

Daniel's eyes were drawn to Lorelei's mouth again, as he recalled the surprisingly erotic kiss they had shared. The niggling little thought that had almost surfaced from his subconscious several times this evening finally broke through.

Lorelei watched in panic as Daniel suddenly leaned forward, and carefully examined the wide mouth Susan had reduced with her make-up magic.

''Lori, you've done something to your lips. They aren't

really thin, are they? They're generous and . . ." His
hands pushed on the table until he was halfway out of his
chair.

"Lori, what in the hell is going . . ." he sputtered.

"Daniel, you've got to listen to me . . ." she pleaded.

They both had started talking at the same time, but
before either completed their sentence, the sound of hys-
terical laughter jerked their attention to the tall, black-
haired man standing by their table.

FOUR

Daniel watched the tuxedo-clad fellow wrap his arms around his stomach, and writhe with uncontrolled mirth. The man sputtered, attempting to say something to Lorelei, who stared up at him in shocked surprise.

"She's done it. Susan . . . Susan has finally done it! Oh, Lori, oh . . . you are so beautiful. Oh . . . ha . . . ha . . . ha! It's killing me . . . your face, it's killing me, darling."

Daniel surged to his feet. Where had this insensitive jerk come from, he wondered. And how could he make fun of Lorelei like this? Maybe this man was her clod of an ex-husband!

A red stain of anger swept up Daniel's neck at the thought. He clenched his fists and prepared to deliver a roundhouse blow to the man who mocked Lorelei.

But just as his hand began its deadly arc, the lady in question jumped between the men and desperately grabbed at Daniel's fist before it could become a lethal weapon.

"No, Daniel . . . stop, don't hit him! This is my friend, Mark . . . Mark Tolliver."

Tolliver. She said Mark Tolliver, not Howard Taylor. As her frenzied words penetrated Daniel's anger, he instantly froze.

When Lorelei felt Daniel's muscles relax under her fingertips, she realized that she had said just the right thing to defuse the situation. Sherman Schreiber must have told Daniel about her friendship with the Tolliver family. Why else would the model have accepted this date?

Yes, that was the question that kept surfacing in Lorelei's brain . . . just why *had* Daniel Logan let himself be pushed into a date with the *matzopunim* Schreiber had described on the phone?

He'd do it to keep you from ruining his modeling career and the agent's business, Lorelei's conscience harshly informed her. And then she remembered the not-so-subtle threat of blackmail she had made to the agent in her nursery office.

That's why Daniel agreed to have dinner with a woman he thought was a pitiful mistake of nature. Yet, except for a few minor slips of the tongue, Lorelei had to admit that he had behaved wonderfully to her all evening long.

Feeling very ashamed of her suspicions, she watched Daniel shake out the tension from his shoulders, offer his hand to Mark, and calmly introduce himself, as if violence had never been threatened.

"Hello there, Mark, I'm Daniel Logan. Won't you join us?" he offered.

Her friend's eyes bounced from Daniel's extended hand, to Lorelei's astonishing visage, and then back to the redhead's sign of peace. Mark's own hand slowly crossed the distance.

"Hi, Daniel, I'm glad to meet you . . ." he began. But his eyes seemed to be irresistibly drawn to the magnet of Lorelei's altered features. The smile that had never quite left his mouth tugged at the ends of his lips. Dropping

Daniel's hand, Mark took hold of her face and turned it back and forth.

"Lori? Susan finally got you to join her drama club, right? Honey, I think someone should have told you that you've forgotten to wash off the make-up. Come on, let's all sit down and you can tell me everything about your part in the play." He reached for an extra chair.

"Mark, no!" Lorelei desperately whispered, glancing over at Daniel. Now that her disguise had been blown, she had some humble apologizing to do. And she couldn't with Mark around. She'd be even more embarrassed.

"You don't have time to sit down, Mark," she protested, while drawing him a little distance away from the table. "Your party must be waiting for you to order. Why don't you go along now, and I'll give you a call tomorrow? I can't wait to hear how the rescue project went. You're back early, aren't you?"

"No, I'm right on time," Mark countered. "I called to invite you out tonight, but all I got was your answering machine."

As he glanced at Daniel Logan, casually leaning against a chair a few feet away, Lorelei saw the good humor lighting Mark's pewter-colored eyes replaced by a hard gleam.

"What are you doing here, Lori?" her friend asked. "And just where did this guy come from?" There was a surprising edge to his voice.

"Oh, this is a . . . a . . . business meeting," Lorelei hastily invented. "I'll explain everything tomorrow, Mark."

Lorelei knew that her voice had risen to higher than its normal level. When Mark just continued to stare at her, she looked around for something to deflect the rampant curiosity she saw in her friend's face. She finally seized upon the room itself.

"You were certainly right about this place. The decor is marvelous." Actually, anything beyond the table was just a fuzzy smudge without her contacts, but Lorelei improvised bravely. "The chandeliers, the wallpaper. And I can't wait to taste the food we've ordered. Oh, thank God, here it is now! Well, goodbye, Mark."

The waiter had arrived with a laden cart.

Mark shook his head, and then waggled a cautionary finger at her as he led her back to her table. "OK, brat. You're the winner of this round, but I'll drag the truth out of you tomorrow, at Susan's place."

"S-Susan's place?". Lorelei stuttered.

"The annual picnic. It's at her home this year, remember? And you'd better be there with a lot of answers." His warning floated back over his shoulder, as he strode across the floor toward his table.

Standing there, watching Mark's retreating form enter the general blur of the room, Lorelei finally realized why her vision was so bad . . . Daniel Logan still had her glasses! She swung around to ask for them, and found herself about three inches away from twinkling hazel eyes.

"Why don't you just retire to the ladies' room, sweetheart? I'll ask the waiter to keep our food warm, while you wash your face." His voice held both humor and an absolute note of command.

Lorelei looked up at him helplessly. "Can I please have my glasses, Daniel? I'll never get there and back without them."

"And have you skip out on me? No, ma'am." He patted his coat pocket, "I'll keep them as collateral for the answers to some questions of my own."

Wordlessly, Lorelei gathered up her purse, and carefully picked her nearsighted way toward the lounge.

It's just as well that she can't see how many people are following her progress across the room, Daniel thought, as he watched Lorelei's lovely bottom negotiate the narrow path between the closely placed tables.

In the sequestered marble elegance of the ladies' restroom, Lorelei Hunt spent five minutes wiping off the persistent shading. Fortunately, the lounge's attendant had produced a small tube of cold cream, or the process would have taken much longer.

As it was, when Lorelei's skin finally came clean, it's natural glow had been enhanced by the prolonged scrubbing. A blush of embarrassment that refused to fade also lingered.

Chagrined by her childish ruse, she nonetheless knew that she had to face Daniel. He deserved an explanation and an apology, at the very least. While Lorelei fished in her purse for her normal make-up, she rehearsed her speech to him under her breath.

"Well, you see, Dan, your agent said I looked as homely as a piece of matzo . . . and I thought that I could hear *you* laughing at me on the other end of the line. And I promised myself that I'd never let another man humiliate me. My husband of eight years dumped me for a perfect souffle . . . and how would you like it if you were called a 'mutt'? You wouldn't, would y . . ."

Lorelei abruptly halted as a party of three women piled into the room, giving her strange looks.

She hastily pulled the pins out of her bun and brushed through the shining length of her hair. Then, digging into her clutch for her cosmetics, Lorelei leaned close enough to the mirror so that her features were in focus. She applied a layer of soft brown mascara to her pale lashes. Feathering her brows with the same shade of pencil defined the wing-shaped arches and drew attention to the large, sapphire eyes that now dominated her face.

Finishing her transformation with delicate pink lip gloss,

Lorelei surveyed the change. For a rush job, it wasn't bad, and at least she looked her normal self again. Taking a deep breath, she tipped the lounge attendant, and then walked back into the dining room.

From his table, Daniel watched heads snap around as Lorelei entered. He recognized the dress—and her lovely figure—but it was hard to believe that this was the same woman who had left ten minutes ago. A surprising surge of possessiveness jolted his body when Lorelei's progress across the room provoked unmistakable stares of masculine appreciation.

Sliding into her chair, Lorelei ducked her head as she repositioned her napkin. But a long-fingered hand reached across the table, lifting her rounded chin until she looked into warm, slightly shocked, green-gold eyes.

"I see that you already know how to emphasize the good points. You are beautiful . . . on the outside, as well as on the inside, Lorelei." Daniel's voice and expression were soft with admiration. But then the heat of his gaze intensified into probing beams as his eyes narrowed. "But why, why did you do all of this?"

Lorelei searched his face, and saw curiosity mingled with a touch of vulnerability. She felt wretched as she realized that she had actually hurt his feelings.

"Oh, Dan, it seemed like such a good idea at the time," she began. "But I knew it was dumb the minute I saw you. I should have called off the date when I saw how sorry you were for me, but I was caught, and . . ."

"Now, just slow down, Lori. You're not making much sense. Take a deep breath and begin again," Daniel advised softly. Any anger he had been feeling seemed to have dissipated during Lorelei's frantic outpouring.

Taking that breath, and collecting her thoughts, Lorelei tried once more. "I overheard your phone conversation with Sherman Schreiber yesterday. I had just gotten soaked in my greenhouse when he arrived, and I know that I looked like a real mess. But then he got on the phone to you, and I heard him insulting me. And you seemed to be as bad as he was. I swear, I could hear you laughing at me on the other end of the line. So I decided to make you both pay for calling my face a piece of matzo!''

"Ah, yes, the infamous *matzopunim*.'' Daniel's smile was full of regret. "Lori, please forgive me. I guess I did laugh, but it was more at Sherm's reaction than at you, believe me. He's really a good guy, and a loyal agent, but he kind of gets carried away by his ideas. He loved your letter, and I was really impressed with it, too. It made me feel glad I was a human being, and not a fool to pose for such nonsense.'' He reached across the table to stroke her soft cheek.

"Lori, I wanted to know the person who could write with such control and delicacy, but I've got commitments on my time you wouldn't believe. So when Sherm suggested the publicity dates, I refused, rather violently. He really got into a panic last night, almost getting down on his knees, begging me to go on this date. I think he's scared to death of you.''

Lorelei grimaced. "Well, I acted very mean to him, more or less threatening him with perpetual ruin,'' she admitted. She went on to detail her relationship with the Tolliver family, and her less than ethical use of them for her revenge.

"I'm also going to have to apologize to Mark and his parents for taking their name in vain, so to speak. They'll all be at our annual picnic tomorrow at Susan's house, and when Mark gets through teasing me, I guess I'll be eating crow all day instead of hotdogs,'' Lorelei laughed.

"Oh, Lori, you are something else,'' Daniel chuckled.

He reached into his pocket and offered Lorelei her glasses. "Here, I think you've earned them back."

"Why don't you hold onto them until we leave?" Lorelei countered. "No more camouflage for me tonight, and anyway, I don't think they'll fit in my purse." She indicated the small bag.

"OK, I'll keep them safe," he agreed, replacing the frames in his breast pocket.

Suddenly feeling very lighthearted, Lorelei demanded, "But tell me, Daniel Logan, just what does a woman have to do for some food in this elegant joint? I'm starved!"

In response to her request, Daniel immediately snapped his fingers and conjured up the attentive waiter, who magically appeared with their postponed meal.

The dinner took them almost two hours to finish. During the meal, Lorelei told Daniel a bit about her *Blooming San Diego* project, and he had her convulsed with laughter relating stories about the modeling business. They were so involved with each other that neither saw Mark wave goodbye when his party left. Nor did they notice the gradual thinning out of the supper crowd.

Finally, the head waiter topped off their coffee for the umpteenth time with a loud harrumph and a significant look at his watch.

"Sir, madame, the cocktail lounge is open until two, and there's dancing in the Lotus Room, if you'd like."

Emerging from their absorbing conversation, Lorelei and Daniel suddenly realized that theirs was the only occupied table, and that the busboys were removing the chairs from the rest for vacuuming.

"A drink, or dancing, Lori?" Daniel asked with a raised eyebrow.

"Oh, I don't know. I love to dance, but perhaps we should be going. It's almost eleven, and you've got a long trip ahead of you, back to L.A., and . . ."

"No, we are not going to end this just yet. I can manage a turn or two around the dance floor," he decided. He rose, and then helped her out of the chair.

How strangely this evening had turned out, Lorelei thought as she got up. Unexpected fires of another sort were replacing the burning anger that had begun the night. Daniel's words—his tone—and the large hand guiding her through the deserted room started dangerous ripples of feeling in Lorelei.

All through the extended meal, she had tried to focus on Daniel Logan, the person. But as they walked into the semi-darkness of the Lotus Room, the potent maleness of the man threatened to swamp her senses.

The Lotus Room hinted at turn-of-the-century China. Gigantic urns, painted screens, and intricate tapestries enclosed the dancing couples in the opulence of the long-ago East.

Daniel led Lorelei onto the floor, settling her into his arms. She sighed as her cheek nestled into the hollow where his strong neck curved into the amazing width of his shoulder.

"The Lamp is Low," Daniel murmured, naming the modernized Ravel piece the band played. As Lorelei came into his arms, he felt emotions so deep and complex it was a wonder that he didn't lose his rhythm and step all over her toes.

Peace and a sense of homecoming vied in his mind and body and heart with a pervasive, all-encompassing desire. As the long, slow tide of music washed over them Daniel was compelled to pull Lorelei closer, until thigh brushed thigh, and his chest found the pillow of her high, firm breasts.

To Lorelei, the whisper of Daniel's ragged breath in her ear became a symphony of subliminal themes. At first, she thought that her own wayward desires were making her imagine the signals he sent her. But when they were jostled by another couple on the crowded floor, he pulled her even closer and she could hardly suppress a cry of surprise.

For, in that instant, the sensual music they had been creating between them coalesced into throbbing awareness. Lorelei felt the need she had been experiencing reflected in the undeniable proof of Daniel's arousal. He wanted her! This beautiful, empathetic man found her attractive, so attractive that he had hardened with desire.

Bemused, Lorelei's eyes locked with Daniel's. Masculine question and feminine affirmation leapt between them in an instant.

But another second after that potent visual exchange, Lorelei shook her head in a fierce, silent "No!" Awash in a sudden wave of vulnerability, she buried her face against Daniel's neck.

He chuckled into her hair, moving callused fingertips under its silken mass to rub her nape. "Coward," he taunted.

But she knew he wasn't angry that she had quixotically accepted, and then immediately rejected, his silent suggestion that they rent a room for the night. And Lorelei was sure she sensed genuine affection in his touch, as he continued to caress her neck. She somehow felt very safe with this man, and that loosened Lorelei's tongue enough for her to say exactly what she had been thinking all evening.

"I certainly hope you never have to earn your living playing poker, Dan," she murmured into his bronzed skin. "I feel like I've been reading your mind all night long. Are all redheads so transparent?"

"Only the natural ones, sweetheart. But don't be so smug." He tilted her chin up. "I'm not having much trouble understanding what's in those beautiful, aquamarine eyes of yours, either," Daniel murmured, as he hugged her fiercely to his body for a telling instant.

Lorelei unhesitatingly returned his embrace with all the pent-up emotion she had had to control since Howard's defection. As her arms tightened around his waist, she rubbed her cheek against his, and deeply inhaled the unique scent radiating from his skin. She had never felt like this in her life. And to think she had almost refused to meet this man!

Daniel shuddered, knowing that he was in danger of losing control for the first time since he was a teen.

"Oh, sweetheart. I think at this point we need a little fresh air," he rasped into her ear. Grabbing Lorelei's hand, he abruptly turned and led her in a path between the swaying couples. Once out of the dimly lit room, he spotted a door conspicuously marked "To The Beach."

Though the night air still contained the lingering warmth of an unusual heat wave, the sea breeze seemed cool and welcome on Lorelei's burning cheeks. She raised her face to the wind as she walked with Daniel down a macadam path to the edge of the cliff on which the hotel was built. Banistered stairs meandered down to the beach. But, in silent agreement, they stayed on the upper path, walking along the crest of the bluff, until they found a look-out that offered both a magnificent sea view and a low, redwood bench.

Beckoning to Lorelei, Daniel pulled her down to sit next to him. He put a warm arm around her shoulders and then rubbed his chin on the pale satin of her hair.

Together, they sat for a long time, breathing in the clean, pungent richness of the sea. They drank in the velvet night that surrounded the indistinct shapes of sloop and dingy, yacht and rowboat tied to the hotel's marina below.

Many of the vessels were lighted, and they bobbed like tethered fireflies on the rolling ocean.

Somewhere out to sea a storm had passed, and now its power was inexorably moving from water molecule to water molecule, advancing even closer to the beach. The soft hiss of tingling foam lapping at the sandy shore slowly built into a mighty boom of powerful breakers.

As if in concert with that gathering force, the gentle caresses Daniel had been sliding over Lorelei's shoulders and arms, the soft kisses he had dropped on her hair, no longer suited the night. He turned her in his arms, and Lorelei gazed up into his moon-shadowed face. The strong angles of his cheekbones were tight with a tension just hinted at in his hazel eyes.

Feeling, need, desire vibrated between them once more. Almost as if they were still dancing, they moved in unison, closer together. Daniel traced Lorelei's features with unsteady fingers. But though his hands trembled, he didn't rush to kiss her. He wanted first to dip into the richness of her hair, to stroke and pet the silken weight of it.

Lorelei moaned as Daniel's lips glided where his fingers had been, brushing along her hairline, skimming across her smooth forehead, to linger with soft caresses on the heated skin of her cheek.

Unable to wait any longer, Lorelei turned her face, compelling Daniel to meet her mouth. Suddenly a taut line of control seemed to snap in him, and he captured her lips with the avid need of a parched man encountering life-saving water. And as his wide mouth came alive, it claimed Lorelei's lips in a kiss which ignited the air around them. The fiery contact banished languor, replacing it with a blazing passion that would always be a cherished memory for the both of them.

"It's taken so long. I've looked for you everywhere, Lorelei. I can't believe I've finally found you." He murmured words that were at once unbelievable yet were ringing with complete sincerity.

One part of Lorelei's brain demanded clarification of his urgent claim, but that sane, questioning islet was quickly submerged. It was replaced by the clamoring of every other cell in her body, as Daniel's mouth ravaged hers in the fiercest, most tender statement of need she had ever imagined.

The kiss in the dining room had been a pale shadow of what he could do with his firm, mobile lips and soft, searching tongue. Lorelei's mouth opened to his male questing, and the invasion drew from her a response beyond any passionate experience she had ever had with Howard.

There was actually no comparison between the devotion Daniel paid to her lips and the self-conscious expertise her former husband had used in his cursory attempts to arouse her before actual lovemaking began.

Slowly, Lorelei learned what caring really meant. This man wanted to please *her!* Without apparent regard for his own needs, he tested, searched, tried to find out just what she liked—what caused her pulse to race and her skin to burn.

Responding to that unselfishness, Lorelei gave of herself as she had never done before. She moaned her pleasure when Daniel found the sensitive spot just under her earlobe. She arched her body against his in wanton reaction when he darted a seeking tongue into the pink shell just above that lobe.

Without words, she praised him for his gentle talents. Groaning, Daniel suddenly pulled Lorelei onto his lap. She wrapped her arms tightly around his chest, and gave into the urge that made her rub against the strength of his loins.

His large hands found her breasts and, as gentle fingers

tugged at the cresting tips, Lorelei felt a simultaneous thrill of ecstasy and a sickening jolt of alarm course through her body.

What was happening to her? How could she be on the brink of losing control with a man whom she had met less than six hours ago? She had only been touched by one other man in twenty-seven years, and now, all she could think of was to shed her confining clothing, and to lie down with Daniel on the soft, fragrant grass.

"We have to stop," she cried, stiffening in his arms.

"This has got to stop," Daniel grated in the same instant. Even as he spoke, he gently moved her away from his lap and put a cooling foot of space between them on the bench. Not daring to look at her, he struggled to dampen down sensations that had almost started a chain reaction.

Lorelei watched as Daniel took one deep breath after another. She would have fled if her own shaking body would have permitted it. But instead, she sat fighting to get enough control to apologize to Daniel for her incredible behavior.

"Another second, and we would have melted these down."

To Lorelei's surprise, instead of shouting at her, Daniel was smiling and holding out her forgotten glasses.

"Oh, Daniel, I'm s-so sorry," Lorelei stuttered, as she accepted the hornrims and jammed them on her nose. "I don't know what happened. All I can do is apologize for letting you get so, and then . . ."

"And I apologize for doing the same thing to you," he interrupted with a husky chuckle.

"Then you're not angry, you don't think that I'm a tease . . ." Lorelei began.

"Never! We both just realized that this is not the time, and certainly not the place," he said, gesturing to the narrow bench on which they sat. "Come on, sweet lady. I'm afraid that we both have got to get home."

Daniel held out his hand. When Lorelei took it after a moment's hesitation, he helped her up from the bench, and then strolled with her back to his Corvette.

Half an hour later, Lorelei inserted her key into the door that led to her apartment. She turned to look one last time at Daniel Logan.

"This has been the most interesting evening of my life," he said, voicing the exact words that played on her own lips.

"For me, too." She nodded her agreement to that understatement. "Well, Daniel, thank you for dinner, and I hope you get everything you want from life."

"I like that sentiment. But it sounds mighty like a good-bye, rather than a goodnight. We'll be seeing each other again, Lori," Daniel assured her.

Lorelei felt a sudden glowing lightness as she heard the promise in his words. "I'd like that. In fact, why don't you come to the annual Tolliver-Hunt picnic tomorrow? Susan would love to have you, and you could meet her husband and my parents and Mark's folks. And we have games and contests, and lots of food . . ."

Lorelei knew she was babbling, but she couldn't stop until Daniel placed a gentle finger on her lips. Feeling totally confused, she gazed up at him.

Daniel didn't know what to say. He wanted to spend more time with Lori, but he had already lost valuable study time and he couldn't jeopardize his grade in Building Materials. Although he was sure he already knew the stuff backwards and forwards, it was one of the most important classes in his major.

"You'll never know how tempting a family picnic sounds, Lori," he finally sighed. "And I'd really enjoy meeting the rest of your family . . . and the Tollivers. But

I honestly don't see how I can make it. I've got a lot to do to prepare for Monday. I'll be free for a while, after I get that commitment out of my way, but as it is . . .''

"Oh, I understand," Lorelei assured him, trying not to sound as dejected as she felt. She had to fight the crazy desire to pull Daniel into her apartment and lock him in with her. Lorelei had the feeling that once he got into his car, he would disappear forever, like some erotic midnight fantasy.

"I *will* call you," he promised, as he took her face between his large hands. His head lowered toward hers, but at the last instant, Daniel forced himself to stop.

Grabbing Lorelei's hand, he dropped a quick, hot kiss on her palm. "I'm sorry. I don't dare taste your mouth again, or I'll never get out of here."

As Daniel bolted for his car and pulled out of her driveway with a farewell wave, Lorelei stood looking after him. She clenched her trembling fingers over the spot on her palm that still tingled from the touch of his lips.

Entering the stairway that led up to her apartment, Lorelei tried to figure out a way to keep from washing her hand until she saw Daniel again.

FIVE

The bee wouldn't go away. Casual shooing and vigorous waving did nothing to deter the insistently buzzing creature.

"I'm not a flower. No nectar to gather here," Lorelei protested, burying her head deeper into the pillow. But the rhythmic humming persisted, until the noise finally penetrated Lorelei's stupor and she recognized it as the unrelenting ring of her bedside telephone.

Groaning, she mildly cursed the insensitive instrument. Lorelei reached a not-too-steady hand for the device and mumbled a rude greeting into the receiver.

"What a way to speak to your one and only sister!" Susan chuckled. "Better not let our parents hear you talk like that. Mom has recovered enough to help Dad wash out your mouth with soap when you get here."

"Get there? What do you mean?" Lorelei muttered, as she swung her legs off the bed.

"To the annual picnic, which begins in two minutes," Susan countered. "And don't tell me that you're not coming. I can't handle the hoard we're expecting by myself." The desperation in her voice sounded authentic.

73

"Oh my God, it's almost noon," Lorelei gasped, as she lifted the bedside clock into focus. "I'll be ready and over there in half an hour. Bye!"

Hanging up the phone, Lorelei dashed for the bathroom. There was no way she could miss this event. The Hunt-Tolliver get-together was into its third decade, and even the supremely independent Mark highlighted it on his calender. The date went in ahead of stockholder meetings, Christmas, and his latest wife's, or mistress's, birthday.

Turning on the shower, Lorelei analyzed the slight sense of depression she felt about going to this year's party. It would be the first time in a dozen years that Howard wouldn't be with her, but that should definitely be a source of relief rather than sadness.

And then she remembered. Last night she had asked Daniel Logan to come to the picnic and he had turned her down. Sweetly, reluctantly—but clearly—he had said that he couldn't make it. How embarrassing to think that she had almost begged him to join her family and friends!

Well, he certainly was under no obligation to her. In fact, Lorelei couldn't think of one reason for him to want to have anything more to do with a woman who had tricked him like she had . . . except for the heated kisses they had shared. But maybe he really hadn't been as affected by them as she had been. Maybe kissing a woman senseless like that was an everyday occurrence in his life.

The more Lorelei thought about it, the angrier she got . . . not with Daniel, but with herself. Forget the power of his kisses, she chided her body as it recalled the taste of his hot mouth and the feel of his strong hands. And even if he called in the future, she'd be a fool to see him again.

Daniel was a fantasy—the perfect man her imagination had constructed out of a compelling picture in the Sunday newspaper. Her business, her book, her degree were the only dreams that she should pursue in the near future.

When the shower had cleansed her of any lingering sense of gloom, Lorelei dried off and pulled on a green bikini. She covered it with cuffed beige walking shorts and a matching sleeveless blouse. Then, inserting her contacts and applying a light layer of waterproof mascara and peach-colored lip gloss, she put the make-up into a small kit to take with her.

Grabbing her terrycloth coverall, purse, and keys, she was in her twelve-year-old Nova and on her way to La Jolla within the promised time limit.

Susan did indeed need help. The population of Hunts and Tollivers seemed to have increased threefold since last year's event . . . and that didn't even include the miscellaneous friends and neighbors who had also been invited.

"Tell me all about last night!" Susan said by way of a greeting. But then, to Lorelei's vast relief, her sister pushed her toward the chaotic kitchen and promptly forgot about her demand.

Lorelei spent the next hour preparing endless plates of hotdogs, hamburgers, and potato salad. A human chain had been set up to try to keep flocks of hungry children and teenagers from imminent starvation.

Finally, Lorelei filled her own plate and managed to escape to the patio without encountering her sister again.

Waving a greeting to her parents, who were already engaged in a cut-throat bridge game with the elder Tollivers, Lorelei found an unoccupied recliner in the shade of a pink-flowering crape myrtle tree. Thinking that her mother looked better than she had in months, she stretched out and took a big bite of the juicy hamburger.

"Well, well, well, the witching hour is over, and our Lorelei is once again transformed into the ravishing beauty we all know and love." Mark Tolliver picked up Lorelei's long legs and draped them over his muscular thighs, as he settled at the other end of the furniture.

"Mark!" Lorelei protested, almost choking on her food when she felt his instantaneous reaction. Folding her legs into an Indian-style pretzel, she tried to dampen the blush that threatened to flood her face.

"Come on, honey, there's nothing to be embarrassed about. Surely you know basic biology, the difference between men and women? And I am nothing more than a man, after all. A man, not your brother, not even your cousin," he gently reminded.

"I know that we're not related," Lorelei agreed.

"Mentally, perhaps, but emotionally?" He sighed. "I didn't have a chance with you, after those first delightful fumblings we shared as teenagers. Howard Taylor moved next door to you, and that was that. Well, he's history now and it's finally my turn with you, Lorelei Hunt!"

Looking into dark gray eyes, Lorelei saw the shocking strength of Mark's demand.

"Your turn?" she asked, her voice full of confusion. "Oh, you're just teasing me, Mark. You don't actually expect me to believe that you've been waiting for me all these years. Why, you've been married twice. In fact, your first wedding was a month before mine. And since then, you've gone through two-thirds of the eligible ladies in San Diego, La Jolla, and Palm Springs!"

"And what does that tell you, except that no other woman has meant anything to me. Damn it, Lorelei, don't you realize that I married those two because they were tall, and blond, and had crystal-blue eyes . . . and for no other reason!" he blurted.

"Oh God, Mark, that's insane! If you really felt like that about me, why didn't you say something back then?" But before he could answer, Lorelei shook her head. "No, even if you had, it wouldn't have changed a thing. Loving Howard was like a virus in my blood. And it took a phone call from his pregnant mistress, to cure me of that particular infection. Talk about stupid . . .''

With shaking hands, Lorelei put her plate with its barely touched hamburger on the ground next to the lounge. But before she could swing her legs off the cushion to escape, Mark grabbed her hands and brought them to his lips.

"Honey, don't go on blaming yourself like this. We all do dumb things when we're in love. Look at me. What's important now is to give *us* a chance. Just give it some time. I won't rush you. I know it'll take some rethinking on your part to see me as anything more than a pal. But I'll wait. With Howard neutralized, I have all the time in the world to become the man in your life.''

Touched by the caring she heard in his voice, Lorelei squeezed his hands, and then settled back in her seat.

"I don't know what to say, Mark. First, I went from being my father's daughter to being Howard's wife. And then I was married so long, and unmarried so quickly. I think that I really need to be free for a while. I've decided to go back to school and finish my degree, no matter how hard it is. So, the last thing I want right now is to fall in love again. I'm going to push myself to my limits and find out who I really am.''

"Well, you can take as long as you need to find yourself, sweetheart,'' he granted. "Just don't shut me out. I understand that you're a one-man woman by nature, and that when you fall in love, it's a lifetime commitment. To be truthful, I'm glad Howard turned out to be such a bastard. He's freed you to love again. So, I'm warning you. I'm going to make damn sure that, when you're ready, I'll be the only man near enough to make any impact on your mind and emotions.''

"Nice of you to give me some notice of your intentions,'' Lorelei chuckled wryly. But that bubble of humor abruptly caught in her throat when an unwanted picture flashed in her brain. She felt a telling flush run across her cheeks, as she suddenly saw herself on a windswept cliff, entangled with Daniel Logan. Lorelei vividly remembered the impact *he* had made on her mind, her emotions . . . and her body.

She abruptly realized that she had never felt such a soul-wrenching, instant attraction for any other man. Not for Howard . . . and not for Mark. Mark had been a life-long friend—her best friend—but his dark good looks had never stirred any feelings in her beyond intellectual appreciation of his handsomeness.

It was doubtful that she would ever see Daniel again, but her reaction to the model convinced her that there was no hope of her ever falling in love with Mark. But how could she keep from hurting him? How could she phrase what she had to tell him and still keep the friendship she treasured?

Ever watchful, and seemingly telepathic where she was concerned, Mark Tolliver groaned. ''Don't tell me that it's already too late! Don't tell me that after one date with that . . . that . . . redhead, you're already taken.''

''T-taken? What do you mean, taken?'' she stuttered her guilt.

''I mean committed to *him*.''

''No! Last night was a one-time affair. I-I mean it wasn't a date, it was just a joke. I have no intention of ever seeing him again,'' Lorelei insisted.

And remembering Daniel's parting ''I'll give you a call,'' she suddenly decided that his farewell statement probably had been the classic male brush-off.

''Some joke!'' Mark said. ''The man was drooling all over you, even while you were in that 'homely' disguise. Where did you meet him, anyway? And what in the hell were you doing at the hotel with him in that get-up? Exactly what was going on last night, Lorelei?''

Several interested pairs of eyes had turned their way. Desperate to keep a few dozen people from coming over to learn every intimate detail of her life, Lorelei immediately related the whole story to Mark. She carefully censored the last part of it, but by stressing the ludicrous aspects of the date, she managed to divert Mark's anger, changing it into wicked appreciation of her revenge.

"Well, Logan and Schreiber certainly had it coming. Imagine that model being so dumb that he couldn't see your beautiful face past the make-up," Mark scoffed.

"Oh, he is anything but dumb." Lorelei found herself defending Daniel. "And he realized that something fishy was going on, even before you saw us. But after your laughing fit, the game was completely blown, and I had to 'fess up."

"Was he mad?"

"Mad? No, he's got a terrific sense of humor," Lorelei admitted.

"God, you had me scared for a minute. I was afraid that because I've been out of town, I missed that small interval in time when you were free of Howard and not committed to someone else. Just remember, Lorelei, some day soon you're going to be mine."

"Mark, no. I'm sorry, but nothing romantic is going to happen between us. Please believe me," Lorelei begged.

But Mark didn't acknowledge her forceful plea. Instead, he grabbed Lorelei's shoulders and pulled her toward him for a fervent hug. Her own arms automatically twined around his neck for balance.

His embrace was so tight that Lorelei didn't have enough air left in her lungs to cry out when her eyes were suddenly drawn to the side gate, and to the latecomer Susan rushed to meet.

"Daniel!" Her sister's delighted voice carried across the yard. "I'm so glad you were able to follow my directions. Welcome to our home."

From her position locked in Mark's arms, Lorelei felt the heat of Daniel Logan's narrowed hazel eyes laser right across the lawn, and burn straight into her soul.

SIX

Buffeted by the shock of Daniel's unexpected arrival, Lorelei felt suddenly paralyzed. Conflicting emotions of joy and fear froze her in Mark's arms, until she realized what this embrace must look like to Daniel.

As a hot surge of blood rushed to her cheeks, Lorelei abruptly pulled away from the dark-haired man who still held her. Mark's confused gray eyes followed her glance over to where Susan was now introducing Daniel to her husband and daughter.

Unable to look away, Lorelei watched as Daniel shook hands with John Grant, and then gravely inspected the autographs on the walking cast protecting seven-year-old Amelia's left leg.

With a profane snarl, Mark pushed up from the chaise longue.

"Never going to see him again, huh? Well, where are your manners, Lori? Come on and say hello to the guest you invited."

"But I *didn't* expect him today. I mean, it is true that I invited him. It was the polite thing to do after he heard us talking about the picnic last night at the hotel. But he said he couldn't come.''

Lorelei was stretching the truth a little, but how could she reveal to Mark that she had almost begged the model to come to the event?

"Well, he changed his mind for some reason," Mark grated, a disgusted look on his face. Turning his back on Lorelei, he stalked over to the Grants.

Reluctantly, she followed behind him. God, her head hurt. There seemed to be a war going on in her brain.

Mark was right about one thing, Daniel *had* changed his mind about coming here today. And to Lorelei it could only mean he had decided that seeing her again was more important than preparing for the commitment he had mentioned last night.

But as thrilled as she felt at the thought, the idea also scared her. Lorelei had meant it when she told Mark that she needed time to pursue her own goals and ambitions. She really didn't feel ready to begin a new relationship with any man.

Yet, when she remembered how Daniel had kissed her last night, avoiding a romantic entanglement with him suddenly seemed impossible. Damn it, she silently swore. What would happen to her, and to all her plans, if she allowed her rampaging hormones to sidetrack her logical brain? Her greatest fear was that she might end up in another one-sided relationship in which she did all the giving.

With the pain in her head reaching monumental proportions, Lorelei watched Mark near Daniel and the Grants. She quickened her step, afraid of what Mark would say to Daniel . . . or what Daniel might reveal to him.

But Mark just slapped Daniel on the back like a long-lost buddy.

"Say there, Dan, my man. Great seeing you again.

Lorelei was waiting for you to get here. Isn't that right, sweetheart?" Mark asked, as she reached the group. He put a possessive arm around her shoulder.

Lorelei felt incapable of saying anything. She was daunted by the look in Daniel's green-gold eyes. They were cold as they swept over her face and came to rest on Mark's hand, which caressed her upper arm.

"Oh, you're wrong, Mark . . . Lori wasn't expecting me," Daniel said. Not expecting me at all, he thought angrily, the vivid picture of her and Mark embracing replaying in his mind. "I was on the freeway, halfway back to L.A., when I changed my mind about coming today. I guess I should have checked with Lori to see if I was still welcome."

"Of course, you're welcome here," Lorelei blurted. And she suddenly realized that, in spite of all her mental reservations, she actually meant what she was saying. "But why didn't you call me last night, or this morning?"

"It was too late by the time I retraced my route," Daniel explained. "So I checked into a motel near your nursery. I was bushed and forgot to ask for a wake-up call. By the time I surfaced and phoned you, I just got your answering machine. Then it dawned on me that you never had a chance to give me directions last night and I didn't have any idea where Susan's house was."

"Well, Dan, I'm glad you found our number and called me for instructions," Susan said.

Lorelei scowled at her sister. Just how long had Susan known that Daniel was coming, she wondered, and why hadn't she said anything?

"I meant to ask you to come to this crazy event, myself," Susan was informing Daniel, "when we talked yesterday in Lori's apartment, but I got . . . sort of sidetracked."

Daniel grinned widely at Susan, remembering his first

reaction to the cosmetic masterpiece she had created on Lori's face. He automatically gave Lorelei a wink, forgetting that he was mad at her.

A surprising wave of happiness passed through Lorelei at the gesture. It showed her that Daniel was a man who didn't stay angry long. How different that was from her experience with Howard, where she had walked around on eggshells for days after an argument.

But Daniel's expression immediately turned grim again when he noticed that Mark's arm was still slung possessively around Lorelei's shoulders.

Seeing the sudden tightening on Daniel's face, and knowing that he must have formed the wrong impression about her relationship with Mark, Lorelei tried to move a step away from her friend. But Mark immediately tightened his grip.

Oh, he can be so stubborn, Lorelei fumed. But not wanting to provoke a confrontation in front of everybody, she couldn't very well jab him in the ribs.

Taking advantage of her predicament, Mark kept Lorelei by his side while he insisted on introducing Daniel to the rest of the adults scattered around the backyard.

"And finally, these remarkably preserved specimens are our parents," Mark said to Daniel, leading the tall model to the wrought-iron table where the bridge tournament still raged.

"Watch that mouth of yours," Jane Tolliver demanded of her son, "or I'll ask John to use his hedge clippers to trim off a disrespectful inch or two from your tongue."

Mark was not fazed by his mother's threat. "Everyone knows that you dote on every word that falls from your one and only son's lips, Mom. But let me introduce a friend of Lorelei's and mine. This is Daniel Logan, everybody. Daniel, my mother, Jane Tolliver. Lori's mom,

Charlotte Hunt. Her father, Admiral Patrick Hunt. And my dad, George Tolliver.''

Lorelei watched as Daniel shook hands with the men and gave the women that to-die-for smile.

"I'm happy to meet all of you," he offered. "After talking with Lorelei last night, I looked forward to getting to know her family . . . and her friends. I know how important you are to her."

Lorelei couldn't keep back the warm glow that invaded her body as she listened to Daniel interact with the people who *were* important to her. He was so charming and at ease with them. He seemed to know just what to say to bring a smile to the lips of the person he was talking to.

"And Mr. Tolliver," he was saying to the publisher, "I hope you don't mind if I tell you that I've really admired the progressive stands your papers have taken on several issues."

"Thank you, my boy," the senior Tolliver replied heartily, not noticing that Mark turned toward Lorelei and covertly made a gesture indicating that Daniel's words were making him gag.

"Looks like we've got a suck-up artist in our midst," Mark whispered in Lorelei's ear.

She frowned, at first not seeing anything wrong in Daniel's expressing his admiration for George Tolliver. The publisher's papers *did* support liberal social and environmental reforms—reforms that she agreed with, and had thought that Mark advocated as well.

But as Daniel went on praising the publications, Lorelei wondered if he wasn't being a shade too reverential to the older man.

The sudden image of Daniel tooling up U.S. 5 toward Los Angeles at two in the morning popped in her mind. What actually had prompted him to make that late-night U-turn? Was it really because he wanted to see her again, or was the prospect of meeting the very powerful George Tolliver the attraction that had pulled Daniel back south?

"Glad to see that our philosophy has some supporters in the younger generation outside our immediate family," George responded to Daniel's accolades. "You wouldn't play bridge, would you, Dan? We're always on the lookout for fresh blood around here."

"I can play. But I'll bet that I'm not in your league," Daniel said.

"Ah, what's happened to American education, today?" the rotund man complained. "Nobody takes time to learn the finer things in life. Mark's hobby is chasing after birds, human and otherwise; Lorelei pots plants; and Susan, here, puts on plays in the local jail. What's your game, Dan?"

"Oh, I've had to work at too many jobs over the years to have time to develop a hobby, sir. But right now I earn my living as a photographic model, and that might seem like a game to a lot of people," he chuckled.

From the look in Mark's eyes, Lorelei was sure that he was going to say something wicked. But before he did, Susan piped up.

"Well, I'm sure that nobody here would think that way," her sister said. "Especially not after they saw the ad you did modeling with that puma."

At the buzz of questions that erupted from the group, Susan explained. "The advertisement was in your Sunday supplement a few months back, Uncle George. Anybody remember it? Daniel posed holding the animal on his back. It must have taken real courage, because the creature looked fearsome!"

"Oh, yes, I remember it well!" Charlotte Hunt enthused. "Tell us all about that assignment, Dan. Were you really on a desert mesa, or was it a backdrop in a studio? I could tell that they used a live cat, I guess one of those hand-raised wild animals you hear about. But even so, how did how did you ever trust that creature enough to let it ride on your back? And what about . . .''

''Mrs. Hunt, stop,'' Daniel pleaded with a chuckle, as he held up a hand to stem the avalanche of questions. ''You're asking me to remember one of the most miserable experiences in my life. But I will tell you that we actually did shoot in Arizona, where I froze my . . . ah, ears off. We also had a crazy photographer, who spent two days taking pictures from a thousand angles while he babbled about the magnificence of the desert light and the strength, of the geologic formations. And as for that damned feline! Well, I still have nightmares about the blasted cat, so please forgive me if I'd rather not discuss the beast.''

''Did it hurt you, did it scratch you?'' Susan breathed.

''No, Susan, the puma never laid a . . . paw . . . on me,'' Dan admitted. ''I know it takes away from the fantasy the photographer created, but the cat was declawed.''

''Then, what did it do to you that was so horrible?'' Lorelei whispered, unable to stifle her concern.

''Lori, it's something I can't even talk about in public. Something that only my future wife will ever find out.''

There! That got her thinking, Daniel observed with satisfaction, as he watched a becoming rush of blood highlight Lorelei's lovely cheekbones.

I had to ask—and he had to tell me—Lorelei chided herself, as everybody laughed at her embarrassment.

''Well, everybody, I think it's time to start the fun and games . . . the picnic variety, that is,'' Patrick Hunt announced in a commanding voice.

''Maybe these young people could supervise this year,'' George Tolliver suggested. ''I've got a hot hand going here.''

''Come on, George,'' Patrick goaded. ''Let's show these kids that we can do more than play cards. I've scheduled the sack race first, then it's the tug-of-war and the three-legged event.''

"All right, Patrick," the publisher gave in. "I guess I should get some blood circulating to my feet. But I'm not going to try to fit into a sack this year. Now, horseshoes is another story. There's a game of skill. Bet I still can whip anyone in the place at horseshoes."

As the older men went off to round up contestants for the sack race, Lorelei looked over at Daniel. She wanted to suggest a walk around the yard, so that she could talk to him for a few minutes. There were several probing questions she had to ask this man.

But as she took a step toward him, Mark grabbed Daniel's arm.

"Say, Logan, let's see if we can beat those young jocks over there in the sack race," he challenged, pointing to where several teenaged boys were shimmying into gunnysacks.

"Sack race . . . haven't thought about them in years," Daniel replied. He quickly glanced at Lorelei. She had been about to say something to him. And he certainly had a lot to say to her, too. But it would have to wait until they had a little privacy. And that was something Mark Tolliver seemed determined to prevent, Daniel acknowledged with a rueful grin.

"Are you game, Logan?" Mark demanded again. "I'm sure Susan and John can find some shorts and a T-shirt for you to wear. Those clothes are too good to ruin."

"Yeah, come on into the house," John offered. "I must have something you can use, Dan."

"OK," Daniel agreed. "Sound's good. Haven't run a sack race since I was ten or twelve. Lori, why don't you meet us over there? You'll want to root for the best man."

Instead of rooting, fifteen minutes later Lorelei found herself wiping tears of laughter out of her eyes. Men over six feet tall had no business competing in this event, she decided. As she watched from the sidelines, Dan stumbled and fell, half a dozen times, until he finally tripped over Mark. Then, as Mark fell, *he* sprawled into the boy next to him. And that started a domino-like chain reaction, which took out most of the contestants.

The men were much more effective in the tug-of-war, but Lorelei still hadn't managed to talk to Daniel. Mark wouldn't leave the two of them alone for a minute.

In desperation, she got someone to call Mark away just before the three-legged race began. Then Lorelei asked Daniel to be her partner. Paradoxically, she hoped for a little privacy with him in the milling, laughing crowd during the practice period.

After they spent a few minutes perfecting the art of walking with their legs tied to each other, Lorelei began to wonder if she had made a mistake. He answered her every attempt to start a conversation with monosyllables.

"You know, we don't have do this," she finally said in exasperation. "You must be tired after getting so little sleep."

"I'm OK," Daniel bit off. He knew that he was behaving like a clod, but he'd been having a hard time getting the picture of Lorelei's and Mark's embrace out of his mind. Instead of dimming, the image had become increasingly vivid in the last hour. And by the time Lori invited him to partner her in this race, his temper was sizzling.

He tried to calm down, but when he finally decided that he had to tell her exactly how he felt, his voice had a cool, hard edge to it.

"Perhaps it's *you* who doesn't want to be my partner, Lorelei. I know that Mark doesn't look too happy over there, either."

Goaded by Daniel's angry words, Lorelei glanced at Mark, who was practicing with Jennifer Klein, one of

Clint's athletic classmates. No, Mark didn't appear to be in the best mood possible, she acknowledged. She had always paired with him for this event in the past.

Well, she hadn't meant to anger or hurt Mark by not competing with him this year, but her friend was behaving like a two-year-old today. And she just couldn't let Daniel go back to Los Angeles this angry . . . or before she had a chance to sort out her conflicting feelings about him.

"He obviously thinks he has a claim on you," Daniel went on. "Maybe I made a mistake when I changed my mind about coming today." *Or maybe Lorelei had realized overnight that Mark Tolliver was a man who could offer her a hell of a lot more than I'll be able to, for a long time to come,* Daniel thought cynically.

"Exactly why you came here is what I want to find out," Lorelei agreed, bringing their forward motion to an awkward stop. "Although I really meant it when I invited you, and I was sorry when you said you couldn't make it, I'm confused about why you changed your mind and drove all that way back last night."

"Yeah, I saw how confused you were when I walked into the backyard," Daniel grated.

"Oh, Dan . . . I know how that clinch must have looked to you. But *I* wasn't hugging Mark. The whole thing was his idea."

"Does Tolliver know that?" Daniel countered, examining her eyes carefully.

"Yes, I've told him how I feel, and he doesn't want to listen," Lorelei admitted. "But whatever Mark thinks he feels for me, we will always be the best of friends—no more and no less."

"And me? Will you always regard me as another . . . friend?"

"A person can never have enough true friends. And I thought that I had found a real one last night."

"Ah, Lori. You did, sweetheart, you did," Daniel said, feeling his anger melt away. "And I'm sorry about getting mad. It's just that I somehow feel very territorial about you, even though I don't have that right. I'm finding it hard to remember that we met less than twenty-four hours ago. And I'm also finding it impossible to think of *you* as just a friend. I want us to be so much more."

"Dan, that's the problem. You have to realize that I've just come out of a painful divorce, and I don't want to be pressured by you or Mark or anyone into something I'm not ready for. I told you about my book and my plans for school. Can you understand that I need to go slow in any relationship that might develop between us?"

"Yeah . . . OK. I guess that I can go along with going slow." *At least until I change your mind,* Daniel thought with a mischievous light warming his eyes. "And to prove it, my good friend, I'll just concentrate on getting to know you and your family better today, and having a grand old time at this picnic. Now, what do you say, shall we dazzle the crowd with our fancy footwork?"

Using their tied-together legs as a pivot, Daniel swung them around in a circle until Lorelei shrieked with laughter.

"Oh, stop. That's enough, my head is spinning," she protested.

Ending the whirling dervish, Daniel held Lorelei closely to him for as long as he dared.

Lorelei stood with her eyes closed, her cheek resting on Daniel's shoulder. If she never had to move from his arms, that would be all right with her. She felt lighthearted and happier than she had in a very long time.

It wasn't until much later that she realized there were several questions she hadn't asked Daniel Logan . . . and that he hadn't even answered the one she *had* put to him.

But now, still feeling slightly euphoric, she impulsively feathered a quick kiss on Daniel's firm jaw.

Expecting that her mouth would touch the smooth, taut skin she remembered from last night, she was not prepared when her lips encountered a thousand tiny pinpricks of pleasure. Lorelei looked up to see the gold glint of new hair on Daniel's face. He hadn't shaved! She speculated on just what it would feel like if Daniel Logan kissed her on every inch of her skin with those erotic whiskers.

God, what was she thinking of? She had just told him that she wanted to go slow, and now there was nothing she'd rather do than be alone with him in her apartment, where she could indulge in every fantasy she had about this man.

Shaking her head in self-disgust, Lorelei forced herself out of Daniel's arms.

Daniel immediately let her go, although it was the last thing he wanted to do. Lorelei had responded so sweetly in his embrace that he had been sure the battle had already been won. But when she suddenly stiffened, Daniel realized that he had a long way to go before he caught his Lorelei.

"I think we need a little more practice," he finally murmured after they stood staring helplessly at each other for a long minute.

When she nodded, he gently nudged her back into their three-legged gait.

It took a minute to regain their rhythm, but soon they were walking together as easily as if they were untied. The way they moved together reminded Lorelei of the synchronous beauty they had shared dancing last night at the Hotel Ramona.

Daniel must have been thinking of the same thing, she realized, when he said, "Too bad we weren't born fifty years ago. Fred and Ginger would have had some real competition.''

Just then, Patrick Hunt called the contestants to the starting line. Standing with their bound legs pressed together and their arms around each other's waists, Lorelei tried to concentrate on getting off to a fast start.

However, she was not very successful. As her father chanted the countdown, she was only aware of how Daniel's hard thigh muscles were flexing against hers, and of how warm and strong his large hand felt on the flare of her hip.

Daniel was having trouble concentrating as well. The breeze kept blowing Lorelei's soft sweet-smelling hair against his cheek. And when he felt the firm press of her breast against his ribs, an immediate stirring tightened his body.

Dear Lord, he prayed, *please let me remember how to walk. Walk? Let me remember how to breathe!*

When Admiral Hunt reached three, the rest of the contestants surged forward. But a measurable instant of time passed before the preoccupied pair realized that the race had begun and they took their first step.

Trailing the pack the whole way, they never made up the distance. The couple reached the finish line weak with helpless laughter.

Forty-five minutes later, Daniel and Mark stood at one end of the pool, waiting to swim against each other in the last heat of the annual Hunt-Tolliver relay race.

Daniel had goodnaturedly accepted Mark's challenge to enter the contest, and after much consultation, Clint, who was in charge of balancing the teams, had pitted them against each other. There was a lot of laughing and back-slapping involved, but it seemed to Lorelei only she understood that, instead of having fun and playing games, these men were seriously testing each other's strengths and weaknesses.

The swimming event always began with novices paddling the width of the pool, and slowly progressed up to the most proficient contenders.

Nearing the end of her own lap, Lorelei desperately fought to keep up with her opponent, fifteen-year-old Jennifer. The young girl churned through the water with amazing power.

Oblivious to the cheering crowd, her lungs on fire, Lorelei found one last burst of energy and touched the wall only a stroke behind Jennifer. Lorelei's teammate, Jeremy, immediately dived into the water, trying to catch Clint, who swam on Jennifer's squad.

Still trying to catch her breath, Lorelei cheered on her own team member. "Come on . . . Jeremy . . . drown him in your wake!"

Although her vision was blurred, Lorelei could see the final adversaries—that gorgeous pair of tall, bronzed-skinned men—waiting for the youngsters to reach them at the opposite end of the long pool. Daniel and Mark had hunched over, and stood with their heads ducked between their outstretched arms, waiting for their heat to begin.

A second later a yell went up from the spectators when Clint raised his arm in victory. His opponent graciously conceded defeat by pushing a wall of water into his best friend's face.

But two mature male bodies had already made a clean slice into the black-bottomed pool. Because he had to wait for Jeremy to touch the wall, Daniel hit the water a bit behind. But even as Lorelei watched, he turned on the power and caught up with Mark. From that point, each man's stroke matched the other's as perfectly as if they were part of a synchronized swimming team.

It seemed fitting to Lorelei that the contest should come

down to these two. In one way or another, Mark and Daniel had played out a game of oneupsmanship since the redheaded model had walked into the Grants' backyard and found Lorelei in Mark's arms.

"Look at them go! We'd better get out of here before they slam into us," Jennifer warned, pushing herself out of the pool.

With a panicky look over her shoulder, Lorelei tried to follow.

"Here, give me your hand," a deep gruff voice suggested.

Automatically reaching toward that promise of rescue, Lorelei felt her father's sea-scarred fingers grab her wrist and pull her out of the water to safety.

"Dad is still a lifesaver, isn't he, Mom?" she quipped, using one of her father's favorite puns.

"Red, orange, or green?" Patrick Hunt asked, giving Lorelei the traditional answer, along with an affectionate hug.

"Look, look, here they come!" Charlotte yelled.

Compelled by the excitement in her mother's voice, Lorelei leaned over the mosaic-tiled coving. But she quickly jumped back as two arms cut one last matching arc through the air, and two palms slapped the wall at precisely the same instant.

The annual Tolliver-Hunt relay race had ended in a dead heat.

Shaking water out of their hair, Mark and Daniel quickly pulled themselves out of the pool. Their team-mates surrounded them, calling out congratulations and initiating "high-five" handclasps.

Lorelei's father put a protective arm around his wife as the crowd surged around them. "Let's get out of this riot and sit down, Charlotte," Patrick suggested, pointing out a picnic table and lawn chairs near the pool. Her mother didn't protest, the pain lines suddenly bracketing her mouth indicating that she had pushed herself too far. Her doctors proudly called her recent triple-bypass heart surgery a complete success, but it had been an arduous experience nonetheless.

Lorelei casually linked arms with her mother and helped her dad settle the small, overly thin woman.

"Oh, here's your cover-up, dear," Charlotte Hunt said, indicating the thick terrycloth robe hanging on the back of her chair. "Put it on. You don't want to get a chill."

"Mom, we're in the middle of a heat wave!" Turning to her father, Lorelei gave a quick, questioning look as she slipped into her robe.

He immediately leaned over and laid a permanently sunbrowned hand on Charlotte's forehead. In a gesture that put a lump in Lorelei's throat, the man who had captained submarines in war gently tucked a wayward strand of grayblonde hair behind his wife's ear.

"Well, you're not running a temperature again," he said gruffly, "but maybe we should go home. I know the doctor okayed this outing, but you've been out of the hospital less than two months."

"Oh, hush, Patrick," Charlotte reproved. The warmth in her eyes countered her brusk tone. "I'm feeling perfectly fine."

"Can I get you some coffee and a piece of cake, Mom? Or how about a nice cup of herbal tea and a hamburger?"

"Now, don't hover over me, Lorelei. You and Susan did enough of that when I came out of the hospital. Why don't you go flirt with those incredibly attractive young men over there? Mark and Daniel have been falling over their feet all afternoon trying to impress you. They're waiting for you to tell them what big strong guys they are," she teased.

"Oh, Mother!" Lorelei groaned in a voice that vividly

recalled her fifteenth year. So *she* wasn't the only one to notice the competition. She wondered how many other people had been watching their antics.

In an effort to mask her embarrassment, Lorelei reached into her beach robe and extracted her small make-up purse. She quickly found the contact lens case inside and inserted them. Then, turning toward the afternoon breeze, she brushed out her rapidly drying hair and plaited it into a loose side braid.

As she clamped the end of the heavy length with a barrette, her gaze settled on the crowd of relay swimmers. A sudden shifting in the group gave Lorelei a clear view of Mark and Daniel, still engaged in a lap-by-lap discussion of the race with their teammates.

Her mother was right. It would be hard to find two more aggressively attractive men anywhere in the country. They were equally tall, equally broad-shouldered, equally handsome.

Mark had a strong, square face, with dark gray eyes and short, curly black hair. But even as she acknowledged his appeal, Mark's presence faded into the background of her senses.

A ray of sunshine had broken through a gathering of late afternoon clouds to highlight Daniel's warm, red-gold coloring. A few prismatic drops of water ran off his shoulders, to rivulet down his chest and meander through the wet hair adorning his skin.

Lorelei clenched her hands, trying to deny that her fingers were dying to make that same journey.

As she watched, Daniel pulled on a T-shirt, and adjusted the plaid swim trunks John Grant had loaned him. He tugged the suit up from where it rode dangerously low on his slim hips. Even as she swallowed hard, imagining just what those trunks covered, Lorelei felt a smile touch her lips.

He should look ridiculous in the loud-patterned, old-fashioned suit. But she was sure that if a photographer snapped a picture of Daniel Logan in his borrowed attire this afternoon, she would be reading in the morning papers that droopy swimming trunks had become the nation's latest craze.

"Best race we've had in years." George Tolliver's booming voice snapped Lorelei out of her preoccupation with the vagaries of high fashion. The tall, white-haired man pushed his rotund body through the crowd. Jane followed behind her husband as he walked toward the Hunts.

Mark and Daniel also gravitated to the picnic area, settling on opposite ends of a bench.

"Dan, you gave me one hell of a race," Mark announced unexpectedly. "I can't remember the last time I felt pushed to the wall like that."

He stretched out a hand, which seemed to take Daniel by surprise for a second. But then Lorelei saw the model flash his patented smile as he thrust out his own hand.

"Thanks, Mark. I agree with you completely. There's nothing like real competition to make winning a prize mean something. The race is always to the swiftest . . . or the smartest."

Daniel shot a quick, hot glance at Lorelei, but she wasn't looking at him; she stood with her eyes squeezed shut. He didn't know what she was thinking, but he had to smile at the peeved expression on her face.

In fact, Lorelei seethed with exasperation. Not only did Daniel seem to love playing with clichés; he also definitely enjoyed provoking Mark. His last statement was really a gauntlet thrown down at Mark's feet.

"And, Susan," Daniel went on, "I want to thank you for your hospitality." Ignoring the sudden glare Lorelei threw at him, Daniel exchanged smiles with her sister. "I've never had so much fun at a picnic, or been in a backyard so well suited for an active family. That's quite a pool you've got, John, almost Olympic size, isn't it? You don't see many home pools built for serious swimming.''

"Oh, John's company did the work," Susan explained.

"So you designed it?" Daniel asked John.

"Yeah, I'm a plumber-turned-landscape contractor," he confessed. "And no wisecracks about plumbers being the only people who can afford to live in La Jolla!"

"Don't tell me people really say that to you," Daniel ribbed.

"Actually, John inherited this house from his grandparents." Susan's hand made a sweep that encompassed the rolling two-acre lot and the rambling Spanish-style house clothed in brilliant red bougainvilla. "Otherwise, this plumber's family would live somewhere a bit more downmarket."

"John, did Susan tell you that the overhead sprinkler in my number one greenhouse disintegrated on Friday?"

Feeling like a fool when everyone turned to look at her, Lorelei forced herself to continue with the nonsequitur. "When Tom stopped by to pick up his paycheck on Friday, he took one look at the mess and muttered what sounded like a dangerous oath in Japanese."

"I don't blame him. It must be a disaster. Well, we knew it would blow sooner or later," John reminded her. "Why don't I come out tomorrow afternoon to see what repairs you need?"

"That would be wonderful, though I dread to think what it will cost. But I can't hold off. There are some really valuable ferns started in there that need to be misted several times a day with warm water. It's almost impossible to do that by hand and keep up with the rest of the schedule."

"I'll see what we can do, Lori. Would tomorrow, sometime after noon, be all right with you?"

"Perfect, John. We were too busy with other work on Saturday to do much in the greenhouse. And I gave Tom a few days off next week to take care of his wife and new baby. But even without his help, I should be able to clean up the mess myself by tomorrow after . . ."

The rest of Lorelei's sentence was lost in the sound of a child wailing piteously nearby. Turning toward the alarming noise, Lorelei discovered that the heart-wrenching sobs came from Amelia, who was in Susan's arms, her face buried on her mother's shoulder.

As she wailed out her grief, Amelia's plaster-encased left leg began swinging in a furious rhythm. The weighted limb became a dangerous weapon as Amelia swung it faster and faster in her agitation.

"Don't cry, honey," Susan desperately soothed, while trying to keep from getting punched in the stomach by her daughter's wayward leg. "I can't understand what the problem is, with you crying like this. Amelia, what's the matter with you?"

The girl finally lifted her head and howled, "I haven't had any fun at all, today! Everybody's been racing and swimming, and I can't even get wet!"

Quickly going over to comfort her niece, Lorelei tried to talk to her while dodging that swinging leg.

"Amelia, I'm sorry that you've had such a miserable day. And I apologize for not telling you sooner how proud I am of you. I heard that you're a real heroine. Your mom told me how brave you were when you broke this leg trying to keep from hitting a dog with your bike."

Moving closer to Susan and Lorelei, Daniel bent down to speak to the little girl in a deep, soothing voice.

"Gosh, I didn't realize that we had a heroine here today. But now that I've heard how you broke your leg,

I certainly think you deserve some sort of award, so *everyone* will know.''

"That's a wonderful idea," Susan hastily agreed when her daughter's eyes brightened at the thought. "But what kind of award could we give Amelia? Some sort of commendation?"

With a sudden inspiration, Daniel reached for a pen from his shirt pocket, only to remember when he patted the fabric covering his chest that he was wearing a borrowed T-shirt.

"Does anybody happen to have a pen or pencil on them?" he asked the gathering.

"Right here," John immediately answered, extracting red, green, and black fine-tipped markers from the "nerd pack" he sported in the pocket of his Hawaiian-style shirt. "Never know when I'll need to write up an estimate," he explained when Daniel raised an amused eyebrow.

"Now, tell me, honeybunch," Daniel said as he turned back to the little girl, "just what kind of dog was it that ran in front of your bike?"

"Oh, it was Barnaby. You know, Mary Beth's dog," she replied, after taking her fingers out of her mouth.

"Mary Beth's dog?" Daniel asked, realizing that this might be a bit harder than he thought. "And just what does Barnaby look like?"

"He's huge!"

"Huge, huh? With green pointy ears and a big red nose," Daniel asked, holding up two of his borrowed pens.

"No! Don't be so silly," the child scoffed. "Barnaby's got long, floppy ears, and a sad, droopy face. And Mary Beth says that he's so smart that he can find people just by smelling their old underwear!"

Daniel ducked his head, desperately trying not to laugh.

And from the muffled sounds Lorelei was making, he guessed that she was having the same problem.

"Well, I think I get the picture, Amelia," he told the girl when he got his face in control again. "How about if I draw you a picture of Barnaby on your cast, to remind everybody of how you saved *him* from getting a broken leg, or worse?"

When the girl nodded enthusiastically, Daniel silently gained Susan's permission to pick up her daughter. Holding out his arms to Amelia, he found she entered them without hesitation.

He seems to have that effect on females of all ages, Lorelei thought as she watched Daniel set her niece on top of the picnic table near Charlotte and Patrick Hunt.

Putting her arm around her mother's shoulders, Lorelei leaned forward to watch as Daniel began drawing. She didn't know what she expected, but it certainly wasn't the exact replica of a bloodhound's mournful face. Her mind buzzed with the sudden realization that Daniel Logan was an extremely talented artist!

"George, George, come over and look at this. You're not going to believe it." Jane tugged at her husband's hand, pulling him closer to watch Daniel work.

Nearby, the Tollivers' son made a sound suspiciously like a snicker. Throwing Mark a quick glance, Lorelei could see that he was not as impressed as his mother was with Daniel's surprising show of artistic talent. The dark-haired man stood watching the activity with his arms folded tightly in front of his chest.

Quickly finishing the animal's likeness, Daniel's flying pen began constructing another picture. A recognizable face instantly took shape. And even with the limited selection of colors available, Daniel captured Amelia's big eyes and button nose with a three-dimensional fullness.

When he completed his work, Lorelei realized that the

dog was positioned so that it looked up at the drawing of the girl. The animal's sad eyes were full of love and gratitude.

With a final flourish of his pens, Daniel lettered a cartoon-like balloon over the dog's head that read, "MY HEROINE!"

"There, all done, sweetheart. And I'm sure if Barnaby could talk, he'd be the first to say that you earned this award because you were so brave."

Standing back, Daniel nervously watched the child examine his work.

Amelia stared at the pictures, and then looked up at Daniel with an expression that Lorelei was afraid mirrored her own.

"Thank you, Daniel. You're wonderful," her niece's high-pitched voice piped.

"We'll frame the drawings when the cast comes off," Susan promised Daniel.

Amelia slid off the picnic bench, her face alive with pleasure. "Mary Beth, Mary Beth, look what Daniel did for me," she shouted across the yard to where a group of youngsters were jumping rope. She took several steps in that direction, but then stopped and ran back to Daniel as fast as her leg allowed.

Tugging at Daniel's T-shirt, she pulled at him until he squatted down to her height. As soon as he was in range, Amelia presented his cheek with a big, wet kiss.

"I love you, Daniel," she announced, before running off to be with her friends.

SEVEN

As the afternoon sun flamed toward the horizon, the picnic finally wound down. By six, only the Tolliver-Hunt contingent—and Daniel Logan—remained. All of the Grants' friends and neighbors had left, except for the young people Clint and Amelia were allowed to invite for dinner.

John rounded up everyone sixteen and under to read them the ground rules for supper. "Now, kids, pizzas just arrived, and we rented the complete *Back to the Future* trilogy. So you can eat your food in the family room and give us old folks some peace."

He stepped aside, just in time to avoid being trampled by the herd of hungry youngsters rushing into the house.

When Susan suddenly flopped down on a chair, Lorelei realized that it was probably the first time her sister had sat down all day.

Several conversations were running at the same time, so Lorelei slipped into the one chair left—unfortunately positioned right between Daniel and Mark. She helped herself to a slice of pizza.

As Lorelei was dealing with the hot and messy slice, Jane Tolliver's voice suddenly rose above the general level of conversation.

"George! George, dear, I've just had the most wonderful idea," she informed her husband. "Now, listen carefully. You saw the marvelous drawings Daniel did for Amelia. Well, why don't you hire him to illustrate Lori's book?"

"Illustrate Lori's book?" the publisher echoed. "Now, why didn't I think of that?"

"Oh, no!" Lorelei blanched, throwing the redhead seated next to her a desperate glance. George Tolliver was famous for making successes from crazy, impulsive ideas like this. Ideas that almost always originated in Jane Tolliver's mind. Uncle George had learned from experience that it paid to hear Jane out.

Trying to swallow the mouthful she was chewing, Lorelei choked when it went down the wrong way.

Daniel immediately shoved his glass of iced tea into her hand.

"Here, drink this," he counseled, rubbing the area between her shoulder blades as she obediently gulped down the soothing liquid.

"Thanks, I'm OK now. No need for the Heimlich maneuver," Lorelei managed to quip after she regained her breath. Daniel's answering smile snared her attention; her eyes hungrily watched his wide mouth curve into a riveting grin.

It was several seconds before Lorelei realized that those firm lips were speaking to her.

"Earth to Lori . . . Earth to Lori. Mrs. Tolliver is trying to ask you something," Daniel said with a chuckle. He watched her dreaming eyes widen and then snap over to the older lady. Maybe Lori was finding it as hard as he was to pay attention to anyone else. Things were looking up, Daniel exalted.

Chagrined that he had caught her gaping at him, Lorelei abruptly turned away from Dan and addressed Mark's mother.

"I'm sorry, Aunt Jane, what were you saying?"

"I wanted your opinion about Daniel doing illustrations for your book."

"Oh! Ah . . . Aunt Jane, using original artwork is a very interesting concept, but I'm afraid it's too late. I'm almost done with the project, and I don't need any . . ."

"Nonsense, Lori. It's never too late for a good idea," Jane said, dismissing her and turning her attention to Daniel. "And what about you, Dan? Wouldn't you like to do the illustrations? You'd be helping Lori and yourself at the same time. Modeling must be great fun, and I'm sure you're paid well enough. But even though men can pose for more years than women, is there any real future in it for you? I think that you should consider using your drawing talent as the cornerstone for a long-term profession."

Even in the midst of her aggravation at Jane Tolliver's interference, Lorelei found herself looking at Daniel Logan as a model. She once again felt the impact of his finely honed body, his chiselled features, the glorious coloring that reminded Lorelei of a perfect summer's day. It seemed incomprehensible to her that Jane could suggest such beauty had a finite ending.

But Daniel seemed to agree with the older woman. "Oh, I realize that my modeling days are strictly limited, Mrs. Tolliver," he genially confirmed. "That's why I'm trying to do as much of it as I can right now. It's the quickest way to finance the career I'm really interested in."

"So, just what are you aiming for?" Mark sneered. "To be a professional gigolo?"

"Mark!" Lorelei immediately jumped to her feet at the cruel remark. She bent over him and jabbed her finger into his chest. "What in the world is wrong with you today? Who do you think you are to say . . ."

"Lori . . . Lorelei."

A deep husky voice stopped her in mid-tirade. When Lorelei turned to face Daniel, he bestowed upon her a smile that she would treasure to the day she died. Its impact loosened her knee joints and made her abruptly sit back down in her chair.

"Thank you, but let it go," Daniel coaxed. Her impassioned desire to defend him gave Daniel more hope than anything Lorelei had said or done all day. But he could handle Mark on his own. His voice became quite deadly when he addressed the other man.

"No, Mark, the life of an . . . escort . . . never had any appeal for me. For one thing, gigolos have notoriously bad health insurance and retirement plans. And while I'll admit to bumming around a lot and working at many jobs that required brawn more than brains, at least my experiences taught me just what is important in life, and what is not.

"I looked around here today and marveled at what Susan and John have created. This sums up what I've learned over the last few years—a family and a home are the only things that really matter to me."

Lorelei was about to go to Daniel, to put her arms around him and rock away the pain she heard in his words. She ached to soothe the longing that caught in his voice. But Daniel's next statement froze her to her chair.

"That's why I've been studying at UCLA's School of Architecture and Industrial Design for the last three years," he said softly. "I don't know if I'll ever be fortunate enough to have a family. But I want to be part of creating homes like this one. After I graduate, and after I serve my apprenticeship, I'm going to specialize in designing affordable and livable houses.''

Lorelei could only gape. In spite of the conversation last night, in spite of his references to the philosophy of architecture and the famous names in the field, she hadn't put two and two together.

He was a student—a long-term student—who was in a demanding program that would take up all of his time and energy for years to come. Just like Howard had been. And she had almost fallen in love with him!

"Say, old man. Would you accept my apology?" Mark stood in front of Daniel. "My remark about your being a paid escort was rude and completely uncalled for. Would you like to take a free crack at my jaw?" He leaned a little forward, offering his unprotected face.

"Ah, no, I don't think so." Daniel declined with a shake of his head. "I'm afraid it wouldn't be a love tap. And while Susan and John are your friends of long standing, and might forgive you a show of bad manners, I'm not about to repay their kindness to me by starting a brawl. So let's just forget it, Mark." He held out his hand.

Although his face turned almost crimson with embarrassment, Mark accepted Daniel's offer of a truce and gave the other man's hand a quick, hard shake.

"So you're going to be an architect, Daniel?" Jane mused, as if the deflected altercation had never happened. "That's a disappointment. Oh, not that you're studying the subject, that's wonderful. But I so wanted you to help with Lori's book."

"Ah, Lori's book." Daniel grinned, amused by Mrs. Tolliver's tenacity. "Didn't you say last night that it was called *Sunny San Diego*, Lorelei?"

"*Blooming . . . Blooming San Diego*," she hissed.

"Of course. Now I remember. I'd like you to tell me

some more about what you want to accomplish with your book.''

His smile faded, and Lorelei could see the intellectual interest in his eyes. She remembered how he had listened to the landscaping lecture on the grounds of the hotel the previous evening. And she found herself anxious to explain the thrust of her book to him.

Nobody, except Uncle George, had even asked her the purpose of writing it. And as she began explaining her project to Daniel, his face and his eyes once again became the focus of her attention, while everyone else faded into the background.

"Several months ago," she began, "a series of events occurred that jolted me out of the humdrum of everyday life." Lorelei shook her head, remembering the triple whammy of death and illness and betrayal.

"Beginning with your grandfather," Daniel murmured. And her mother's heart problems, following on the heels of Howard Taylor's infidelity. Lorelei's shoulders had to be far stronger than they looked, to have held up under such a concentration of troubles, Daniel thought, as he examined her pain-shadowed face.

After a second or two, Lorelei nodded to Daniel. "Anyway, after Granddad passed away, I found myself taking long walks through city parks and along ocean beaches. I really needed to soak up all of nature's beauty. I wanted to find order and a sense of purpose again.

"But I slowly noticed that most of the other people walking near me hardly took time to look around them. They didn't seem to care that clouds came in a dozen types and an infinite number of shapes. Or that the rocks and stones under their feet were made up of many different minerals, some as beautiful and interesting as polished gems.

"And I suddenly realized that most folks tend to ignore

the miracles of our world unless they're jarred in some way.''

"You're right, honey," Charlotte Hunt broke in. "It wasn't until after my surgery that I started going out to our backyard to watch the sunrise and sunset. We've had that marvelous view all the years we've lived in Coronado, but I ignored thousands of beautiful moments.''

"Exactly, Mom," Lorelei said, giving her mother a loving smile, before letting her attention encompass the whole group once more. "And I think we all need a little shaking up. That's what I hope the book will do, in a pleasant way. I want to goad people into looking around everywhere they go. I want them to see that nature, and their neighbors, and even the City of San Diego have provided them with an almost limitless array of beautiful and interesting flowers. And hopefully, once people become used to looking for lovely plants, they'll open their senses to the sea, and the sky, and the whole magic universe.''

There was a moment's silence as the gathering digested Lorelei's impassioned vision for her book.

"Mrs. Tolliver," Daniel's voice finally broke the quiet. "Mrs. Tolliver, thank you for suggesting that I become part of such an important project.'' He then turned to her husband.

"Mr. Tolliver, if you agree, I'd really like to try my hand at illustrating Lorelei's book. After tomorrow my schedule is free for a couple weeks. None of the classes I needed were offered in summer school, and I'm not committed to any modeling assignments for a bit.''

Why in the world was Daniel Logan asking Uncle George for permission to work on her *book?* Lorelei fumed, all her recent feelings of comradeship abruptly dissolving.

It should be her decision to ask for any help she might

need. And no matter how much the idea of working with Daniel might appeal to her, now that she knew he was involved in such a time-consuming curriculum, Lorelei didn't want him to become part of her project.

If he did, he would have to work by her side for days on end. And what would happen to her, if during that time she fell irreversibly in love with Daniel?

Lorelei freely admitted that she was so attracted to the man she seemed to have absolutely no resistance to the sensual power he wielded over her. No, she couldn't ask him to assist her with the book . . . she didn't dare.

But before Lorelei could voice her decision, Mark broke in with a collaboration plan of his own.

"Mom, Dad, thanks for the suggestion, but there's no need for Dan to help Lori with her illustrations," he announced. "There's no need at all . . . because *I'm* going to do them!"

"You?" The world was a blending of half dozen surprised voices.

His mother recovered first, though a frown grooved her forehead. "Mark, dear, as proud as I am of you, I have to tell you that your drawing ability never has gone much beyond the 'horsie' and 'doggie' stage."

"No, of course I know that I don't draw, Mom. I never even tried," Mark said in exasperation. "I meant photographs. You know I've had dozens of pictures published from the work I've been doing in the Sierra mountains. Our group documents everything about the life cycle of endangered birds, and I've been taking the pictures. You remember that, don't you, Lori?"

Lorelei nodded. Truthfully, he was a fine photographer. But she didn't want Mark's help, although not for the same reasons she was afraid of Daniel serving as a contributor.

She couldn't help glancing at Daniel out of the corner

of her eye. It proved to be a mistake. Just looking at that strong, chiseled profile generated waves of longing in her that weakened her resolve. The idea that Daniel might stay for a while in San Diego to work with her was so very tempting.

Yet, how could she live with herself if she let another man deflect her from her goals? Oh, Daniel wouldn't be the money-grubber Howard had been; he probably made triple or quadruple her yearly income. But Daniel might destroy her plans in another, more damaging way.

Lorelei felt sure that if he was around long enough, her attraction to him could easily grow into a love so consuming that nothing else in the world would be as important to her as pleasing Daniel Logan.

She didn't dare get so involved. Involvement would mean spending time with Daniel, and he might demand that she come to Los Angeles with him, maybe permanently. That would require her giving up everything for him—even her self-respect!

No, she had made a vow with herself never to let that happen again. So there was no way that she could work with Daniel on the book. However, as Lorelei surfaced from her troubled thoughts, he was pressing for the position.

"Well, what do you say, Mr. Tolliver, am I hired?" he asked.

Daniel hated being pushy, but he really needed the opening this job could give him. If only Tolliver would make up his mind. But he could understand that it was hard for a man to choose between pleasing his wife or disappointing his son.

"You know, sir," Daniel goaded in desperation as the publisher's gaze bounced between Mark and himself, "something like Lori's project would be great on my resume. Who would you rather employ . . . somebody who's illustrated a best-selling book or a guy that can carry a wild cat around on his back?''

George laughed with Daniel at the verbal image the model painted, but then the older man bent down to talk quietly with his wife when she tugged at his hand.

Realizing that her own hands were clenched into fists, Lorelei tried to relax them, while mentally replaying Daniel's last statement. She wondered why he had to be one of that rare breed of people who can laugh at themselves. For all his kidding around, even Mark lacked that trait.

But one characteristic she knew Mark Tolliver did possess was determination. And Lorelei hoped that he would use that talent to help convince his father that Daniel's artistic services were not needed. She had no doubt that once Daniel left for Los Angeles, Mark would quickly forget about helping her.

Her reading of Mark's nature was confirmed when he jumped back into the conversation. "Come on, Dan," Mark cajoled. "I'm sure Lori is grateful for the offer, but it wouldn't be practical. You're based in L.A. Transportation and motel expenses in the San Diego area for the next week or so would cost you more than you'd earn."

"Oh, he can stay with us," Susan put in, grinning mischievously when both Mark and Lorelei glared at her.

"I thank you from the bottom of my heart," Daniel said, bowing to his prospective hostess.

"But *I* wanted to do the illustrations," Mark protested.

Geez, he sounds more like someone Amelia's age than his own, Lorelei thought, trying to keep her mouth from curving in amusement.

"Well, I think it's the perfect solution, Jane!" George Tolliver loudly announced to his wife, after breaking off their whispered conference.

Having gotten everyone's attention, George cleared his throat and addressed his son. "Mark, hold on a minute.

Here's a plan that should make everybody happy. Why don't *both* you and Dan go around with Lori, take pictures, make sketches—whatever? And then I'll pick the best pieces. I'll give you both a fair price for your work, and I'll also pay your working expenses."

Now, this was getting seriously out of hand, Lorelei thought. She was going put a stop to it . . . immediately!

"Uncle George, thank you very much for your offer," she said sweetly, "but really, none of this is necessary. You know I planned to use photo agencies to provide me with stock pictures. They'll have illustrations for most of the well-known places I'm putting in my book. And I've been taking photos of the offbeat locations myself."

"No, my dear, I don't think so. While stock photos can be excellent, I want something unique, like line drawings or watercolors, which I'm sure Daniel can do. And though I'm certain that you're a good amateur photographer, Lori, I'm hiring you for your writing ability. You know that Mark has done some very fine camera work over the years. He's going to be busy supervising our new ad agency after next week, but I don't see why we can't take advantage of his talents for a few days. Just remember, I want quality in your book . . . or nothing at all."

Lorelei could see her plans for the writing project, for the new greenhouse sprinkler, for school—for everything—smashed to pieces by the firm decision she heard in the publisher's words.

Scowling at the two tall men who had put her in this position, she gritted her teeth and said in a small, bleak voice, "Then I guess I don't have much choice in the matter, do I, Uncle George?"

"Now, don't take it that way, Lori," he said, his tone cajoling. "I'm just trying to do the best for everybody. We want something original, something that will make all of us a lot of money. And make us proud, too, let's not forget about being proud.''

"Well, tell us what you decide tomorrow, Lorelei,'' Charlotte Hunt's soothing voice interrupted the confrontation. "Your father and I have to get home. He has to feed and walk Charlie Brown, and I want to put my legs up. They look like something you'd expect to see on an elephant.''

"Mom, do you want me to come spend some time with you?'' Lorelei said anxiously, noting that her mother's legs indeed looked swollen.

"Lori, this is all very normal. Since they took leg veins for the bypass, it'll take a while for the fluids circulating there to find another route,'' her mother said stoically.

"I know, but I worry.''

"Not to worry, my dear. I just have to take it easy for a few more months. Your father does a great job of giving me orders to rest. He used to frighten the young seamen on his submarines with that same voice,'' she laughed, giving her husband a pat on the arm.

"Well, what's left for a retired sea dog to do, but order his wife around and take care of the pets?''

"Why not write the story of your command experiences?'' George Tolliver suggested. "Not too many men served in World War II, Korea, *and* Viet Nam. Not to mention teaching and planning coursework at the Antisubmarine Warfare School. You could call it, ah . . . how about, 'Something's not Kosher Here: The Confessions of a Pigboat Commander.' ''

"I don't think that title would help it sell, George,'' Jane Tolliver dryly informed her husband. "But you know, Charlotte, perhaps Patrick should take on the project. He's entertained us with so many sea yarns over the years. And while he gets a rough draft going, why don't you let me treat you to a few weeks in the most wonderful new spa that's opened up? Besides the usual diet and exercise facilities, this one even has a cosmetic surgery program. We could get a nip here or a tuck there.''

"Oh, you and your spas, Jane. I'll bet you've tried every one of the dozens around San Diego. But it does sound very tempting,'' Charlotte mused. "Maybe they can do something about the zipper on my chest.''

"You have a zipper on your chest?'' Daniel blurted, and then felt his face flame to match his hair when he realized that he had put his foot in his mouth yet again.

But Charlotte just patted his hot cheek. "Yes, dear. You heard that I recently had heart surgery,'' she remarked. "Well, would you believe that they use metal staples to close the incision these days, instead of thread? As I said, it looks just like a giant zipper.''

"Oh, don't worry, my dear,'' Patrick cut in, "those marks will fade in time. And while I agree with Jane that a rest at a spa would do you good, I draw the line at you doing something to change the woman I love.''

EIGHT

The picnic ended with that tender declaration.

After kissing her parents goodbye, Lorelei stayed a few minutes to help Susan with the last of the cleaning up.

"I don't know when I've ever had a more stressful day," Lorelei confided to her sister while they stood in the laundry room folding the mountain of towels that had just come out of the dryer.

"Yes, yes, I agree, there's nothing so aggravating as having two of the most gorgeous men in the country fighting over your affections! God, I feel so old when I realize that nothing like that is ever going to happen to me again. Again? What am I saying, it never happened to me . . . ever!"

Lorelei couldn't help laughing at the expression on her sister's face. But after a minute, she sobered. "Well, instead of being flattered, I still feel like I was drawn and quartered by them today. Who would have thought that two of civilization's finest would act like cavemen fighting over a tasty bone? Of course, I don't know Daniel very well, but I've never seen Mark act that way before."

Susan shook her head, adding another towel to the growing pile in her hamper. "I'll reserve judgment on Daniel, but I believe that Mark *thinks* he's in love with you . . . maybe because of what you represent to him."

"I don't understand, Suzie. What could I represent to him?"

"Let's just say that Mark is going through an . . . identity crisis. I think he's tired of life in the 'fast lane,' and you symbolize the innocence of his youth, and family stability in general."

"Identity crisis? Well, I guess we all have to go through a painful crisis or two, or we wouldn't be human," Lorelei said to her sister in a mild voice.

"Oh, honey," Susan replied, touching her cheek. "Don't worry about being hurt by another man. I think there's one around who's going to make you very happy for the rest of your life."

Susan wouldn't say another word on the subject, but Lorelei mulled over her sister's prediction after she bid her goodnight, and then started down the sidewalk toward her car. Lord, she was afraid that she would have a whole lot to think about in the next few days, with both Daniel and Mark helping to illustrate the book.

As if mentally voicing their names had conjured up the pair, Lorelei found the two men lounging against her car fender. They had helped John clean up, while she was working with Susan.

Both men straightened to their full height when they noticed her approaching the ancient white Nova.

"So, where do you plan to go first, Lori?" Mark asked.

"Home," she said, purposefully misunderstanding the question.

"No, I mean to do the illustrations for your book."

Sighing, she outlined her plans. "Most of the research is done already. I've been to Old Town and the Mission

San Diego de Alcalá. Over the last month, I've driven through residential neighborhoods and found some really spectacular flowers in local parks and green areas. And this week I want to tie everything up by surveying Point Loma, the Zoo, and as much of the rest of Balboa Park as possible."

When neither man said anything, she looked between them hopefully. "Of course, I'll understand if you can't make it. This doesn't give either of you two busy men enough notice to rearrange your schedules. But don't worry. I'll continue taking my own photos and talk Uncle George around somehow."

"Lori, I'm surprised at you, trying to renege on a contract like that," Daniel chided. Now that he had a legitimate reason to be near her for the next several days, he wasn't about to let her wiggle out of the arrangement.

"Contract? I didn't sign anything about using you two in my work."

"You agreed, verbally, in front of a whole lot of witnesses," he countered.

"And you know that verbal contracts are just as binding as written ones," Mark put in.

"All right, all right, both of you. We'll start tomorrow. . . ."

"Ah, tomorrow's no good," the men said in the same breath.

"I'll be finalizing our ad agency acquisition tomorrow," Mark put in. He suddenly stared at Daniel, a strange look clouding his features.

"And I've got a final exam," Daniel said, and then frowned when Mark Tolliver glared at him.

"Look guys," Lorelei began, after seeing the dark visual exchange, "this isn't going to work. I told you my schedule, and . . ."

"But you aren't free tomorrow, either," Daniel reminded

her. "You asked John to look at your greenhouse in the early afternoon."

Lorelei felt like kicking something, or someone. He was absolutely right. She had to get work started on that blasted sprinkler system or lose a valuable crop of ferns.

"Tuesday?" She groaned the question.

"I'm free Tuesday and pretty reasonable for the rest of the week," Daniel said, grinning.

"Me, too," Mark echoed, trying not to be bested.

"Well, I'm never free, except for you, Lori . . ."

"Just what I need, punsters. I should sic my dad on you both. OK, Tuesday it is."

"Tuesday," two baritones repeated.

"Early," she warned.

"I'll be at your place at ten, nine . . . ah, eight," Daniel rapidly amended when he saw the look in her eyes.

"Yeah, early, that's good," Mark put in. "Ah, Lori, could I talk to you about something personal for a minute?" He glanced over at Daniel. "Sorry, old man, I need her advice on something."

"No problem," Daniel said, as he waved goodbye with a negligent hand. "Besides, I just remembered that I have to arrange a few things with John and Susan. Be seeing you soon." *Sooner than you think*, Daniel said to himself as he retraced the path to the house.

When Daniel disappeared, Lorelei finally turned to Mark. But she still saw an image of the model's strong shoulders and perfect backside in her mind's eye. *That man looks just as good going as coming*, she thought wryly.

"You wanted to ask me something, Mark?" she queried when her vision cleared a few seconds later.

"What I really want to do is warn you about some*one*. I've had my suspicions all day long, but now I'm certain I know what his game is."

"Game?" Lorelei echoed, a sudden cold chill playing down her spine.

"Yeah . . . con game. Don't tell me you didn't notice how our redheaded friend's face lit up every time my dad and I talked about our new advertising agency?"

"No," Lorelei said after a moment's thought, "I can't say that I did. What is your point, Mark?"

"My point is, guard your jewelry and gold fillings with this guy. After Howard, you don't need to get involved with another leech."

"Mark, I don't know exactly what top male models make, but the man doesn't need any money from me. He knows how I live, what kind of junk heap I drive. Do you honestly think he's accepted this illustrating job to hit me up for the couple of thousand or so bucks I've got in the bank?"

"Oh, there are leeches, and then there are leeches. What I think he's really after is for you to put in a good word with Dad, for him and this Schreiber fellow. You heard Logan earlier. What did he say? Something about modeling to earn as much as he can, as fast as he can, in order to put himself through school. What better way to cut back the time he has to model than by tying in with the new Tolliver ad agency? We could direct a ton of premium assignments to the man and all Schreiber's other clients."

"Mark . . . Mark . . ." But Lorelei couldn't say anything else. Mark's idea made sense if Daniel really was the type of man to use people. He certainly knows how to charm them, she thought, suddenly remembering the way he had captivated the Grants, along with her parents and the elder Tollivers, the minute he was introduced to them.

Oh, she felt terribly confused. Howard had made her

so unsure of herself . . . so wary about trusting her own instincts.

Abruptly opening her car in a daze of uncertainty, Lorelei got in and purposefully rolled up her car window to cut off anything else Mark had to say. She had more than enough to think about as it was. Gunning the engine, she waved a distracted goodbye to him and drove off.

Lorelei had wanted to make an early night of it, so that she could get up at dawn and finish cleaning up the greenhouse. But after wandering around the confines of her small apartment for ten or fifteen minutes, thinking about what Mark had implied, she acknowledged that going to bed right then would be futile.

Instead, she changed into grubby work clothes and made for Greenhouse One. A couple of hours hard work should allow her to sleep deeply until the morning.

Turning on the overhead lights in the cement and glass structure, she walked the aisles between the banks of raised beds where seedlings and starters of a wide variety of tropical plants were growing.

This greenhouse was devoted to plants that needed high humidity and warmth to germinate and thrive. The ferns were the most demanding in their requirements. Lorelei started them from spores, buying the rarest and most expensive varieties available in glass tubes that held millions of the almost microscopic dots. It was hard to believe such tiny beginnings could yield ferns that might be tree-sized as adults.

Lorelei ran several tests for temperature and humidity. She then checked that the plastic film covering the most recent starter trays was still securely tightened around the edges.

Sighing, she took a push broom out of the corner where she kept a set of tools and began sweeping. The place was a mess. The sprinkler's flooding had left damaged leaves everywhere. And mounds of soil had been washed over the edges of the raised beds, onto the concrete walks that separated the aisles.

She had worked for fifteen minutes when a car door slammed nearby. The crunch of footsteps on gravel made her pause. A push broom wasn't much of a deterrent to a robber or vandal, but she really wasn't worried. The barbed wire that topped her ten-foot fence would keep out almost any kind of trouble.

"Lori," a deep voice called. "Lori, it's Daniel. Please open up."

Lorelei groaned. That tall fence did absolutely nothing to guard her against the husky appeal in Daniel's deep voice. She actually took a step toward the door before stopping herself. How could she deal with the attraction she felt for Daniel while all these doubts she had about him were going round and round in her brain?

Maybe she could pretend that she wasn't here, that the lights were on by accident, that she had gone to a movie.

"Lori, I know you're inside," the husky voice informed her, "I can see your outline through the glass, and I know that you can hear me because the ventilation louvres are open. Come on, honey, I've . . . ah, I've got a message for you from Susan."

Defeated, Lorelei went outside and crossed the few steps to the gate. She knew that Daniel would think of some good reason why he couldn't deliver the information from her sister through the chainlink gate, so she didn't give him the satisfaction of asking. Without even looking up at him, she punched in the required code that opened the electronic lock.

Then Lorelei turned her back on him and retraced her steps to the steamy greenhouse. Picking up the broom, she resumed her work.

When he didn't say anything for long minutes, Lorelei

sighed and asked in a tired voice, "So, what is Susan's message?"

"I'm sorry, Lori. She didn't send me here. I lied. I wanted to talk to you, and I knew that when you had a chance to think about what happened at the picnic today, you'd be too angry with me to let me in any other way."

"But I'm not angry with you, Dan."

Lorelei finally turned and looked at him. The mist in the air softened his features, making him look younger and very vulnerable. Unable to bear the thought that this must have been how Daniel had looked as a lost, lonely boy, Lorelei put her head down and stared at her scuffed Nikes.

"Yes, you must be angry," he countered. "And why not? I pushed myself into your family picnic, I goaded Mark all day, and then I finessed a job out of his father."

At that confession, her head snapped up. Was he really admitting that he wanted to work for the Tolliver ad agency? Then Lorelei realized that he must be talking about doing the illustrations for her book. Although, for all she knew, that assignment might just be his opening to a more profitable association with the Tollivers.

Lorelei gripped the handle of the push broom harder and watched her knuckles turn white. She really didn't know what to think. In spite of what Mark had said earlier, somehow, she couldn't envision Daniel Logan acting in such a devious manner. But maybe she was only fooling herself . . . like she had with Howard for so many years.

Yet, even if Mark was completely wrong—even if Daniel really didn't want to use her to advance his career— the one thing she did know about him was that the pursuit of his future vocation was supremely important to him. And what was the point of starting a relationship when Daniel Logan was just as obsessed with becoming an architect as she was with finishing her degree in ornamental horticulture?

The only way she could allow herself to become serious about someone while she was still in school would be if that person wanted to support *her* for a change. He would have to be able to sacrifice his own needs, for a while, so that she could finally accomplish her goals.

Oh, she didn't need monetary support; she'd handle that part of her education on her own. But if she went into another relationship now, it would have to be with someone who could provide moral support, encouragement, a simple backrub when she needed it. Not someone who was fixated on pursuing his own agenda.

When Lorelei finally looked up, Daniel stood there, still patiently waiting for some response from her. And she suddenly remembered the good parts of the hours they had spent together last night and today. Even if Daniel couldn't fit into her life as it was now, she really didn't want to make him go away thinking that she was mad at him.

"Dan, please believe me, you didn't do anything hurtful to me by coming to the picnic . . . you were invited," she finally said. "If anyone should be angry, it's you, because *I* was the one who tricked you into that farce of a date last night. In order to punish you and your agent, I put on a childish disguise and tried to embarrass you in front of all those people at the hotel."

"Lori, I understand how you felt. You were upset with Sherm and me. I know we must have sounded like rude and chauvinistic bastards on the phone. So, I don't blame you for trying to trick me. But I thought that we had gotten beyond that . . . last night."

"Listen, Dan. Last night you turned out to be someone special, and you transported me to a wonderful fantasy world for a few hours. But today I realized that the joke

I pulled on you didn't have all that much to do with you or Schreiber laughing about my face.

"Although he'll never know it, I really was trying to get back at my ex-husband. And I used you to avenge myself for a wound that Howard inflicted."

Daniel stood there for a long second, looking into her eyes. Lorelei knew that tears were brimming behind her lids. She willed them not to fall.

He put out a hand, wanting to caress her soft skin and ease away the pain he saw in her features, but he dared not touch her until she gave him permission.

Letting his hand drop when she said nothing, Daniel whispered, "I'm sorry the bastard put you through such agony, Lorelei, and that I did anything to add to it."

With effort, he tore his gaze away from her and looked around the ruined greenhouse carefully for the first time. He almost groaned when he saw the extent of the damage. Lorelei had endured so much in the last year—her grandfather's death, her husband's betrayal, her mother's illness—and his own roundabout smashing of her tender feelings.

While Daniel examined the shattered piping, he made a vow with himself to do everything he could to make the next six months of Lorelei Hunt's life a whole lot better than the last half dozen had been.

With plans already formulating in his mind, he spied another broom in a near corner. Tossing a cheerful salute and grin to Lorelei, Daniel retrieved the cleaning implement. Starting at the opposite end of the structure from where she had been working, he began sweeping the debris into a large pile.

Watching Daniel's casual expertise with the broom, Lorelei realized that she didn't have the heart to argue any more. Instead, quietly accepting his help and his comforting presence, she went back to work.

The two of them labored silently for an hour in the

moist, damp heat, slowly reducing the havoc the faulty sprinkler had created. Finally, they filled the last trash bag and Daniel lifted it into the garbage dumpster.

"I'll have to be going, now, Lori," he said, after they exited the greenhouse into the breezy San Diego night. "I have that blasted final tomorrow afternoon."

Looking at his sweat-drenched shirt and pants, Lorelei protested, "You'll catch a chill if you let those clothes dry on you. Come on up to my apartment and take a shower. God, you've ruined your good outfit!" she said, suddenly noticing just what he was wearing.

"It doesn't matter, Lori," Daniel began.

"Of course, it does. Those clothes must have cost a fortune. Well, at least I can iron the pants dry, and run the shirt through the quick-wash cycle. Then, if you're hungry again, after all the work you've done, I'll make you a sandwich to eat while the shirt dries."

"Thank you, sweetheart, I'll take you up on everything. And I'm going to add kindness and efficiency to that list of famous genetic traits that run in the Hunt family," Daniel commented, following Lorelei up to the apartment over the retail store.

Lorelei offered him a seat in the kitchen and a cold drink before she quickly rounded up towels and an old bathrobe that had belonged to her grandfather. Handing them to Daniel, she took an instinctive step backward when his eyes roamed her face and body.

But the thoughts he voiced were definitely not lecherous. "I have a better idea," he said. "You look as bedraggled as I do, and should get out of those wet things, too. So, you take the first shower. While you're in it, I'll change into the robe and run my shirt through the wash. Then, I take my shower, and you can make the food and iron my pants."

Too tired to fight over which plan was the most logical,

she just said, "The washer and dryer are behind that door next to the refrigerator. There's detergent on the shelf. Use the lowest water setting and about a quarter cup of soap."

"I have done a few loads of wash in my day," Daniel said mildly.

"Glad to hear it," Lorelei muttered as she left him.

Going into her bedroom, she locked the door and also secured the one to the *en suite* bathroom. Her soggy jeans and shirt landed in a heap outside the stall shower. Turning on the faucet, Lorelei tried to forget the man in the kitchen by offering up her tense body to the curative powers of hot water.

She washed quickly, and then pulled on fresh clothing. With her hair still wrapped in a towel, Lorelei returned to the kitchen. Daniel sat at the table in her grandfather's robe, busily making drawings on one of her notepads.

"It's all yours. I'll get that sandwich ready while you're showering. What are you doing there?" she asked casually, not able to see much without her contacts in.

"Oh, just doodling, nothing important," he said. But he gathered up the pad and took it with him into the bathroom, along with the bath towels Lorelei had laid out for him.

Wondering at his odd behavior, Lorelei went to the refrigerator and discovered some leftover roast. She quickly put together a beef and cheese sandwich, covering it so that the bread wouldn't dry out before Daniel could eat it.

While putting the ingredients back in the refrigerator, she heard the washer complete its cycle. Tossing Daniel's shirt into the dryer, she set it for permanent press. Using a cool iron and a cloth, she quickly ironed the dampness out of his dress pants.

Finishing those tasks, Lorelei felt strangely restless. She

wiped crumbs off the kitchen table, and then looked around the rest of the multi-purpose room. She didn't spend enough time in this tiny apartment for it to get messy. Nothing was out of place, except for yesterday's newspapers strewn on the floor by the couch.

Lorelei stacked the papers on the coffee table in front of the Danish-modern sofa. Right out of the fifties, the thick beige cushions rested on a slatted walnut frame. The sofa was a little shabby, but long enough and still comfortable enough that it regularly lulled her to sleep when she tried watching a late movie on television.

She realized that the apartment was still very much her grandfather's abode. But it didn't seem worth the effort to start a redecorating project. She had already used up too many of her ideas on the apartment she had shared with Howard. But she had left every stick of that carefully planned furniture behind.

Except for the two dozen plants scattered around the room, she had brought nothing out of her marriage. What would Daniel think of this furniture, and the heavy, masculine bedroom set? He was so sensitive to the atmosphere of a room, a building. Would he realize that she only marked time here?

Abruptly shaking her head, Lorelei told herself it didn't matter what Daniel thought about her living arrangements. The shower was still running, so she decided to do something with her hair. Retrieving her brush from the dresser, she suddenly realized that the blow dryer was in the cabinet in the bathroom.

"Oh, great. Well, at least I can get the tangles out," she muttered to herself. Plopping down on the edge of her bed, she leaned forward and ran the brush through the worst of the snarls.

She hadn't finished half of her hair before a painful spasm ran down her right arm. Rubbing the offending muscles with her left hand didn't seem to help. It was that old shoulder injury acting up again. Lorelei tried to recall the techniques the physical therapist had taught her a few years ago when she had overworked her shoulder by transplanting dozens of small trees in one day.

Spreading her towel on the pillow, Lorelei placed her damp head against the terrycloth and ran through the relaxation exercises. Closing her eyes, she concentrated on visualizing each muscle. She then encouraged the individual fiber tissues to let go and unclench. Bit by bit, the pain slowly left her arm.

And all the while the sound of the shower droned on. The guy certainly likes to get clean, she thought to herself as her eyes fluttered shut.

The brush felt so good. The tug of the bristles through her hair was slow and gentle and sensuous. At the least bit of resistance, long, strong fingers eased through the tangle, lovingly separating the interwoven strands until the path for the brush opened again.

Purring in contentment, Lorelei nestled deeper into the terrycloth. But when firm, gentle lips tugged at the lobe of her ear, and a warm, moist tongue stroked along the outer shell, Lorelei's eyes snapped open abruptly.

She suddenly realized that she wasn't having a delightfully sensuous dream. She actually was locked in the dangerous confines of Daniel Logan's arms. And instead of burrowing into her pillow, as she thought, her nose nuzzled into the robe covering his tanned skin.

Struggling to get up, Lorelei winced in pain.

"Whoa, there, Lori. Don't move. You're getting this brush all tangled."

"What are you doing here?" she demanded.

"Brushing your hair," he explained with utter reasonableness.

"I know you're brushing my hair, but why? Who asked you to brush my hair?"

"No one, but you were tossing in your sleep, and I could see what a mess it would be if it dried like this. Now, just hold it a minute, I've almost got the brush out."

Lorelei was trapped, she couldn't move until he freed the brush, and the longer he took, the less she wanted to leave. They were stretched out on the bed, with the whole length of his body pressed tightly against hers. One of his legs anchored her to the mattress. No doubt if she called him on the compromising position, he would say that it gave him better leverage.

So Lorelei didn't protest, even when he pulled her closer to him and revealed that not all his concentration centered on removing the brush from her hair.

"There, that's it," he said with satisfaction. "Do you want me to finish untangling it?"

It was an offer she couldn't refuse. At the reluctant nod of her head, Daniel chuckled and began working again.

Slowly, Lorelei could feel him making some progress. He developed a technique in which the hand holding the brush would stroke down, the fingers of his other hand would gently separate the strands, and then he would readjust their bodies so he could reach another section.

"OK, I'm done with the right side, turn your head so I can reach the left. No, that's too awkward for you," he decided. "You'll have to move over here."

Daniel tugged on the belt loops of her jeans, indicating that he wanted her to swing over him and lie on the other side of the bed.

And without listening to the frantic warnings of her brain, her body responded. But somewhere in the process of moving across his lean form, he stopped tugging . . . and Lorelei stopped moving.

Her whole body rested on top of his. The sides of his robe had almost separated, and she felt the damp heat of his skin through the thin material of her shirt. The thicker barrier of her jeans did nothing to hide the warmth radiating from where their hips pressed together. A pulsing pressure built at the point of their most intimate fusion. Jolted by the force of Daniel's arousal, Lorelei finally tried to get away, pushing with her hands against the bed on either side of his head.

"Please don't go, Lorelei. Don't leave me," he murmured as both of his hands captured her nape. And then he slowly, insistently tugged downward, until her mouth met his. The slight murmur of protest her mind directed from her vocal cords quickly submerged in a vibrating wave of purring pleasure.

She had forgotten how good he tasted! How could she have forgotten his taste in the short time since she had last dipped deeply into his hot, moist mouth?

Forgetting her doubts about Daniel, turning off her mind and its stern warnings that this man was dangerous to her well-being, Lorelei opened herself up to her emotions.

She encircled his shoulders with her arms, and brought her sensitive breasts into fusing contact with his hard chest as their kiss went on and on. It changed in texture, in heat, in depth with each passing second. And Lorelei never wanted it to end. But she suddenly needed more of him than a kiss. Letting go of him, her fingers frantically tugged at the tie that barely held the robe together. When it was free, she quickly pulled the garment off his shoulders.

As the material fell away, Daniel reached up to run his hands through Lorelei's hair and down her back. He quickly undid the buttons of her shirt and released the metal closure of her jeans. They both worked to shimmy the fabric down her legs.

When her slender beauty was completely bare to him,

he reveled in the silken feel of her firm breasts. Her gasp of pleasure when he stroked their rigid peaks sent an answering surge of delight to his loins.

He stroked and explored and offered his own body to her inquisitive examination, until he could stand the waiting no longer. Cupping her thighs, he nestled his maleness tightly against the heated apex of her femininity.

At the feel of his readiness, Lorelei shook her head in her agitation. But her desire must have blazed from her eyes, as with a moan of desperation, Daniel dug his heels into the mattress. He pushed until he had moved himself into a sitting position against the headboard of the bed.

Daniel reached for Lorelei and pulled her to sit astride his hips, so that they faced each other, lips inches apart, eyes focused on each other's emotions.

Lorelei knew that her eyes must be filled with the same longing she saw in his. And she did nothing to stop him as he slowly raised her hips and impaled her on the throbbing strength of his need.

A low, satisfied moan rebounded around the room. It was made up of equal parts of male and feminine desire. Kissing Lorelei deeply, delving his tongue into the hot recesses of her mouth, he moved his hips and pushed up as far as he could. She responded by first welcoming him into her moist softness, and then by clinging tightly to him when he withdrew a little.

With her hands gripping his shoulders for support, Lorelei rode on and on, until shimmering waves of intense pleasure jolted into her body with each new cantering motion. But just before the journey to the realm of joy ended, a strong hand gently lifted her chin, and her untiring mount called to her.

"Look at me, Lori," Daniel's soft, strangled voice choked. "Look at *me*!"

Eyelids reluctantly fluttered open and confused blue irises looked into demanding hazel.

"Good," his voice encouraged. "Now tell me, *who* do you see?"

"Who? Y-you, I see you, D-Daniel," she stammered, hardly able to articulate at all.

"Damned right! It's me, Daniel. Remember, there's only me . . . and never . . . anyone else again."

His hands closed harder around her thighs, lifting, guiding, setting a faster rhythm that Lorelei quickly learned, and then matched. The heat, the need, grew again.

And all the while Daniel's eyes never left hers. The bronze-green irises compelled and watched every change on her face. But those honest eyes were also open to her, and Lorelei saw everything he felt as well.

His gaze never faltered, never glazed, even when the tumult came—to him, to her—and ecstasy blazed between them. But instead of dissipating, each individual wave of pleasure, male and female, joined and blended, sending an even higher surge of rapture raging through both their bodies.

Lorelei collapsed on Daniel's chest, sobbing. She didn't know why making love to him should have created this deluge. She didn't cry easily. Even Howard and all his antics had prompted anger more readily than tears. Lorelei hadn't even cried last January when she heard Howard on the phone telling Carol that he was "going to get rid of the graceless frump" he had married.

Howard had hung up and then he had seen Lorelei standing in the doorway. For an instant the usual cheerful expression on his face slipped, and for one terrible second Lorelei thought that he had meant he wanted to kill her.

"Sweetheart, what's the matter?"

Daniel's concerned question recalled Lorelei from the distasteful memory.

"Lori, you're trembling. Are you cold? Did I hurt you? Darling, please stop crying . . . you're tearing my heart out."

He gathered her into his arms, tucking her against him and pulling the cover over both of them.

Lorelei knew she was shaking, but it wasn't from cold. "I didn't want to do this," she finally stopped sobbing long enough to articulate.

"No, sweetheart, neither did I. We didn't want to make love with each other any more than we want to eat or breathe." He chuckled softly, while soothing a hand through her hair. "But that's how it goes. And now that we've started, making love is going to be as vital to our well-being as either of those necessities."

"But, Daniel, don't you remember that we didn't even know each other before six o'clock yesterday? What kind of woman—what kind of man—does something like this? I can't believe that I couldn't stop myself."

When she felt the tears begin a slow trickle once more, Lorelei rolled away from Daniel. She pulled open a drawer in the bedside table and yanked out a wad of tissues from a box stored there.

"Hush, now, just hush, sweetheart," Daniel's voice caressed, as she tried to wipe away the salty flow. "No more talk like that. You have nothing to be ashamed about."

Sitting next to her on the edge of the bed, he tilted up her chin a little, until he could look directly into her eyes. When she had difficulty meeting his probing gaze, Daniel's large hands moved to her shoulders, and gave her body a gentle shake.

"Now, look at me and listen carefully to the truth, Lorelei. You wanted to know what kind of man I am . . . well, I'll tell you. First and foremost, I am *not* promiscuous. I've never had a one-night stand in my life. Even when my hormones ran wild as a teen, I controlled myself. My worst nightmare was the thought of a girl leaving a baby of mine in a trashcan for the garbage collectors to find.''

That stopped Lorelei's tears instantly. She gasped at his bluntness, and then reached out to touch his cheek softly, trying to ease away the pain of abandonment that she saw on his face.

Sighing, he turned his mouth into her palm and pressed a kiss into her lifeline. ''Lori, what I mean is that I've had only a few relationships and I can't remember the last time I was with a woman.''

''Well, you'll be relieved to know that you haven't forgotten any of the steps,'' Lorelei murmured. The flippant words hid the shock she felt at Daniel's revelation. She would have thought that he could claim dozens and dozens of lovers.

Yet she couldn't help being delighted, both by the fact that he had been so discriminating, and by the shout of laughter that rose out of Daniel's strong throat at her feeble jest.

When he gave her earlobe a playful tug, Lorelei smiled faintly. But then she tried to respond to Daniel's honesty with equal candor.

''Dan, I guess I should tell you that I was completely faithful in my marriage, and that I haven't been with anyone else since my separation.''

''Lord, I knew you were a bawdy wench! Two men in twenty-seven years . . . shocking,'' he teased, but a tender smile formed on his lips.

''Oh, Daniel, I know that I haven't led a wild life. But I still feel that I behaved irresponsibly tonight. I can only promise myself that this will not happen again. I am not going to make love with you or anybody else until at least the latter half of the decade, and even then . . .''

Lorelei stopped speaking as Daniel suddenly wrapped his arms around his stomach and rolled onto his back.

"Daniel . . . what's the matter." Lorelei questioned anxiously. But then she got a good look at his face and shouted, "Daniel, how dare you! Daniel, stop laughing at me this minute! I really meant what I said. You have to understand that there's no room in my near future for any man, not even one I like and respect and desire as much as I do you."

"How can you say that, Lori?" Daniel asked, after he recovered from his laughing fit and finally coaxed her back into his arms. "I can see us liking and respecting and desiring each other for all the years to come. Lori, don't you remember what I said to you last night on the cliff outside the hotel?"

She shook her head, but his words instantly came back to her.

"Yes, you do," he countered, as if reading her mind. "You remember when I said that I've been looking for you for a long time. And I have. Only you're more perfect than I ever dreamed."

His fingers traced around each full breast before spanning the dip of her waist and then caressing the flare of her hips.

"Oh, I knew you would be tall and slender," Daniel said softly, as Lorelei fought the flood of heat that his words and hands provoked.

"But in reality, Lorelei," he continued, "your body is incredible. And so is your hair. I imagined that you might be blond, but how could I have known this would be made of pure gold?" He ran his fingers through the soft strands he had worked so hard to free after her shower.

Lorelei couldn't help giving a little moan of pleasure. She should stop the flow of honey from his lips, but what woman wouldn't want to listen to this kind of talk for hours? Her arms went around his neck as Daniel continued to describe his ideal woman.

"Of course, there was one really big surprise about you. I didn't realize that my dream wife would spend a significant portion of her life digging in manure."

"Daniel! That's not very nice. How . . . how would you like . . ." Sputtering to a stop, she pushed him away. But almost as quickly, Lorelei found herself laughing at the verbal picture he had drawn.

Daniel chuckled, too, and then held his arms out to her. This time she went into them without any fuss. Holding her close to his chest for a minute, his deep voice then rumbled in her ear. "Do you want to know the exact instant I fell in love with you, Lori?"

"When?" she couldn't help asking in a small voice.

"It happened just after we got the salad course in the hotel dining room."

"But, you still thought . . . you didn't know . . ." Lorelei began.

"Yes, it was during the salad," Daniel repeated, as if he hadn't heard her confusion. "I had just put a forkful of lettuce in my mouth when it dawned on me that I had finally found you, even though Susan's make-up job made me think that the love of my life had come to me in a plain wrapper."

Lorelei didn't know whether to laugh or cry at his words, but she found herself shaking her head, sending long blond hair whipping around his shoulders. "No, I'm afraid you're wrong. I am not the love of your life, Daniel. And you're trying to fit me into a puzzle that doesn't match the shape I want *my* life to take."

"Lori, listen. I know we have to work out a lot of details to mesh our complicated schedules. But the bottom line is very simple. Sometime soon you will realize that you are the kind of woman who takes a man to her bed *only* because she is in love with him. I don't know if it happened during the salad, but I am certain that you fell in love with me last night, just as I fell in love with you."

"Oh, Dan . . . Daniel . . ."

"No, don't say anything more, my Lorelei. Just keep touching me like you're doing, and your body and my body will say everything that's important."

Lorelei looked down to where her hand rested on Daniel's muscled thigh. She suddenly realized that, in her agitation, her fingers had been stroking the red-gold hair that dusted his firm skin. Her actions had had a definite affect on both his body and hers.

When Daniel abruptly pulled her under him and thrust deeply into her, Lorelei was as ready as he was for the quickly escalating passion that enveloped them.

Around midnight, Daniel stirred. Lorelei vaguely protested when he unwound her arms from his waist and neck.

"I know, sweetheart, I didn't want to let you go either. But I've got to get back to L.A. Professor Borkin won't take my falling in love as an excuse for missing his final exam in Building Materials. Don't worry, I'll be back at eight sharp on Tuesday," he promised, giving her bottom a loving pat.

Lorelei propped open an eye to watch Daniel dress. She never realized that a man could look so sexy putting *on* his clothes. But she finally remembered that she should protest his return.

As he finished buttoning his shirt, she muttered, "Don't come back to San Diego, Daniel. You're wasting your time. I can't marry you . . . I have this terrible allergy to long-term university students."

He froze for a second, but then just smiled. "That's OK, sweetheart. I hear that some allergies respond to desensitizing therapy. I'll just work on giving you all the exposure you need until you're cured of the malady.''

Groaning, Lorelei turned her back on him. She didn't respond when he covered her with the blanket, or react to the light kiss he placed on her shoulder.

But then she ruined her show of indifference.

"Dan, drive carefully, and good luck on your final exam," she called loudly, just before the bedroom door closed.

NINE

Monday passed in a blur of work and decisions. Lorelei handled a steady stream of customers, almost forgetting that John Grant was supposed to inspect her damaged greenhouse until he appeared at noon. She turned over the cash register to her young assistant Julie and led John to the structure.

He clucked and shook his head while he inspected the ruined sprinkler system. As he walked along the raised cement beds, John questioned Lorelei about the cultivation requirements of the tropical babies she had started there. Then he got on a twelve-foot ladder and checked the corroded piping strung over the beds. When he finally tested the control box that directed the sprinkling cycle, he looked even more glum.

"Nothing is salvageable. Nothing," he muttered. "And even at wholesale prices, a new system is going to run into five significant figures," he warned.

Lorelei felt the blood leave her face. She had counted on John patching here and there, with maybe two or three hundred dollars' worth of repairs. But a whole new system

141

was out of the question, even when she finished the San Diego book and got the rest of her advance.

Suddenly remembering what she had found that morning, she turned to her brother-in-law. "John, come to the office. I'll get you some coffee, and I've got something there I'd like to show you."

Earlier in the morning, Lorelei had discovered the pad Daniel had doodled on the previous evening propped up on the kitchen table. On the first page, he had written: "This is only a preliminary sketch, but show it to John when he gets here. I love you very much, Dan."

After holding the pad to her chest for a long minute, while her feelings threatened to get out of control, Lorelei finally looked at the other pages. Daniel had made a rough sketch of the greenhouse, penciling in an ingenious new sprinkler system. On another page, he had drawn up a list of the required materials.

Extracting the sheets of paper from the top drawer of her desk, Lorelei handed the drawings to John. "What do you think of these?" she asked.

He leafed slowly through the pages. Then digging out his calculator, he did some rapid punching of buttons.

"I'll be damned. This is brilliant!" He whistled through his front teeth. "Lori, you are a genius. I need a more detailed plan, but I think this is going to save you thousands of dollars. I know you've started taking landscaping, but I didn't realize you were so advanced."

"No, I'm not . . . and I didn't design this system."

"Oh, then Tom must have . . ."

"No, Tom's mind has been on his new daughter, not this mess," Lorelei broke in. "Daniel Logan did the plan."

"Dan? Yeah, that makes sense. He'd have the background, studying architecture. I looked into it a long time ago and decided it was too much schooling for me. You have to be an artist, scientist, and engineer all in one. That's why the bachelor's degree takes five years. Then you have to apprentice out for a pittance, and if you want a master's . . ."

"Stop, John, stop! I get the idea," Lorelei said, trying not to shudder.

She suddenly felt a sense of overwhelming depression. And she didn't need years of psychology courses to know that depression was frozen anger.

And yes, she was angry at Daniel Logan for being so perfect. But somehow, she would resist the pull of his physical beauty, his brilliant intellect, and his wonderful sense of humor.

Lord, it wasn't fair! She'd have to be a billion-year-old stone to fight the pull of all that perfection. But she had to do it. No matter how loveable he was, she was *not* going to fall for him. She couldn't bear the thought that another man she loved might reach his heart's desire at the expense of her own. Lorelei knew how selfish and small-minded that sounded, even in the privacy of her own mind. But she didn't care. She had already been down that road and ended up as the butt of an eight-year-old joke.

After almost a decade of marriage, Howard had literally told her, "My, dear, now that you've had the opportunity of working so hard to put me through school, I'm going to let you do the same thing for yourself!"

Well, she didn't mind doing everything for herself. She was completely capable of financing her own schooling and reaching her own goals. She didn't need alimony from Howard, she didn't need a handout from the Tollivers, and she certainly didn't need to marry Daniel Logan.

It was in that frame of mind that Lorelei met her terrible twosome on Tuesday morning.

Daniel arrived first.

"Hello," Lorelei coolly greeted him, as he got out of his leased Corvette.

"Good morning, darlin'," Daniel said, smiling down at her. God, he'd missed her. It was hard to believe that it had only been a day since he had last seen her . . . all tousled and rosy from their lovemaking.

Lorelei watched as Daniel's warm eyes skimmed her sweatshirt and faded jeans, an outfit that mirrored his own.

"You're looking as fresh and energetic as one of Clint's classmates," he said. "Maybe it was a good thing that I was in L.A. last night. That way we both got some uninterrupted sleep in preparation for today's outing."

Her fists clenched at his provocative teasing, but before she could put them to good use, her conscience reminded her that she owed Daniel a word of thanks.

"I showed John the preliminary drawings you did for the sprinkler system. He said that you're a genius and that your design will save me thousands of dollars. I really appreciate that, and I'd like to reimburse you for your work. If you'll send me a bill, I'll . . ."

"Lorelei Hunt."

He said her name with such dark menace that the rest of her sentence died on her lips. Looking up into his eyes, Lorelei saw a strange mixture of messages. It seemed that he was furious and amused in equal parts. Amusement won out.

"Ah, my stubborn little siren, fighting the inevitable to the last. Not that I'm worried about the final outcome. But we'll have to discuss the wedding later," he informed her, as Mark drove up, squealing a bright red jeep to an abrupt stop next to them.

"Hey, Mark," Daniel hailed him. "That's an awesome machine you've got there. A Limited Edition, I see." He ran his finger along the thin gold trim line. "Did you buy it from some teenager who got in over his head with insurance payments?''

''What?'' A puzzled line grooved between Mark's eyes as he got out of the vehicle. ''Oh, you mean the raised suspension looks like something a kid altered and put on balloon tires. The wheels are a bit oversized, but I go over all sorts of terrain where the added clearance makes all the difference.'' He gave the jeep's roof a loving pat.

''Well, hi there, Lori,'' Mark said, as he turned to her with a belated greeting. ''What's in the basket?''

She looked down at the large wicker hamper at her side. ''Our lunch and my equipment. Where do you want me to stow it?''

''Here, I'll put it in with my stuff,'' he glanced into the rear of the vehicle.

Lorelei also looked into the back and saw that the seat bench had been folded down to make room for mounds of hiking and photographic paraphernalia.

''Whoa . . . seems that I forgot to clean this up since my last Sierra trip,'' Mark announced the obvious. ''And this basket's going to take up the last square inch of space. Guess you'll have to follow behind us in your 'Vette, Dan.''

''No problem,'' Daniel shrugged. ''Although, since I'm new to the area, I might get lost. So why doesn't Lorelei . . .''

''Oh, I'm sure Mark will drive slow enough for you to follow,'' she interrupted, appalled at the thought of sharing the close confines of Daniel's sports car with him.

While Mark stowed the heavy hamper, she hurried to the passenger side, avoiding any eye contact with Daniel.

But her refusal to ride with him didn't seem to have made him angry. In fact, he cheerfully offered to help her into the raised jeep when she failed to make it on her first try.

"No, that's all right, I can do it," she declined sharply. Lorelei didn't want him touching her. If he did, she just might turn around and cling to him as if her life depended upon it.

Reaching for the grip above the door, she finally pulled herself into the vehicle, bumping her head on the rearview mirror in the process. With a relieved sigh, she settled into the bucket seat and fastened her safety belt.

A warm gust of air stirred the hair on the back of her neck, as Daniel leaned over to whisper in her ear.

"You are a chicken," he taunted. He knew that Lorelei was running scared, and he felt sorry about the stress he was causing her. But not enough to back away from pursuing his goal.

A hard hand rested on her shoulder long enough to deliver a gentle squeeze. Just a phantom impression of Daniel's strong fingers remained a second later, when Mark hopped into the driver's seat and slammed his door. He pulled his safari shorts into a more comfortable position, and then readjusted the rearview mirror.

"See you at the Point, Dan. I'll keep an eye out for you on the freeway," he promised.

Daniel just grinned, his hand forming a quick salute before he turned and got into his own vehicle.

How could you be so rude to Daniel? Lorelei's tweaking conscience asked. Dammit, I have to protect myself, she responded. But her alter ego didn't even bother to answer that feeble excuse.

Pulling out of the nursery's parking lot, Mark headed for the nearby freeway ramp. After merging with the rush-hour traffic slowly flowing south, he glanced at Lorelei, and then nervously cleared his throat.

"Ah, you know, Lori, I've been thinking. This Logan guy is going to stay at your sister's home most of this week, and what do we really know about him? How about if I get this private detective I . . ."

"Don't you dare say another word, Mark Tolliver," Lorelei broke in, shaking with a sudden savage anger she had never felt before. "If I find out that you've done something so underhanded, I will never speak to you again . . . ever."

Mark's face abruptly lost its deep tan. And when his color returned a second later, there was a red cast highlighting his skin.

"All right, honey, all right. It was just a suggestion."

Hoping to keep Mark from proposing yet other malicious idea, Lorelei turned her head to stare at the passing landscape. But for once she didn't even notice how beautifully the heavy roadside plantings of oleander and bottlebrush softened the busy highway.

Instead, her eyes kept checking the side mirror for a midnight-blue Corvette. She needn't have worried. Every time she looked, Daniel was there, tailing them easily in the commuter traffic.

It was just after nine when the mini-convoy passed through the gates that separated the residential part of the Point Loma peninsula from government property, and the national park at its tip.

The second Mark stopped in the parking lot of the visitor's center, Lorelei released her seat belt and was out the door. She waited for Daniel to exit his car, determined to make up for her previous behavior.

"Welcome to the Cabrillo National Monument," she greeted him with resolute cheerfulness. "That statue over there commemorates the explorer Juan Rodrigues Cabrillo's first sighting of this land in 1542. His fellow Portuguese sent the sculpture as a gift . . . like the French did with the Statue of Liberty. But, I've read that more people come to see Cabrillo each year than visit the Lady."

Daniel looked down at the beautiful blond woman who had suddenly turned into a walking guide book. His mouth twitched with amusement. One thing he knew for sure: if he ever caught his Lorelei, life would never be boring.

He decided to play along and become the quintessential tourist. "I'm completely confused. Why were those guys back there at the gate in navy uniform? I was expecting to see a park ranger, not the military."

"Look around you," Lorelei gestured widely. "This peninsula guards the entrance to San Diego Bay. The naval fleet and commercial ships all have to pass here to get to the docks."

"National security," Daniel mused. "That makes sense. I'm surprised the navy even lets civilians down here."

"I'm sure the top brass feel the same way, but there's too much history tied to the point . . ."

"Well, let's get to work, everybody," Mark interrupted, appearing at their side with various photographic devices hanging from his neck, and Lorelei's hamper in his hand. "What do you want me to shoot first, Lori? The plants there around the monument or the flower beds up at the lighthouse?"

But a soft trilling coming out of the jeep interrupted Lorelei before she could explain her plan of action.

"Damn it, I told them not to call me unless it was an emergency," Mark said, stomping back to the driver's side of the jeep.

Lorelei watched as he picked up the cellular phone and barked a greeting into the receiver. She only caught a word or two of Mark's side of the conversation, but by the way he was waving his free hand about, she knew that a crisis must have occurred.

The sudden thought of her mother and a relapse popped

into her head. Hurrying around the jeep, Lorelei reached the door just as Mark hung up.

"Damn, damn, damn," he was muttering.

"Mark, what's wrong? Is . . . is someone sick? Is it your father, or . . ."

"No, angel, nothing like that," he quickly reassured her. "There's a problem with the ad agency we're acquiring. Seems that their lawyers used their electron microscope to find a sub-clause in a sub-paragraph that needs clarification. And since Dad went out of town, our lawyers want me there to initial any changes. I've got to go right now."

"Damn shame," Daniel said, coming up to Lorelei's side. He didn't even try to keep his mouth straight. All he could think of was having Lorelei to himself for several hours.

"Yeah, real stinking shame," Mark agreed, glaring at his rival. "And knowing those guys, they'll find someway to tie me up for the rest of the day. I'm sorry, Lori. Do you want to do this some other time?"

Having seen the satisfied grin on Daniel's face, Lorelei *was* tempted to postpone this research trip. But then she remembered how important it was to finish the book and get the rest of her advance.

"No, I have to keep to my schedule," she abruptly decided. "Come back if you can, but I don't expect this will take too long." An hour, at most, she promised herself.

"Well, in any event, I'll make certain to be available tomorrow. What's on the agenda?"

"The Zoo," Lorelei reminded him. "Be at my place about eight-thirty. Ah, Mark, before you go, could you do me a favor? I didn't bring my own camera, since your father was so adamant about you doing the photography. Would you lend me one of yours for today?"

Mark looked torn for a second, obviously worried about leaving one of his babies in someone else's care. "OK, sure. This one is set for close-ups. And it's idiot-proof. I mean that I use it in situations when both my hands aren't free. Don't drop it," he advised, before tearing out of the parking lot, oversized tires squealing.

With Mark's departure, Lorelei felt a strange mixture of anticipation and dread steal over her. Perhaps it was the conflicting emotions, but she spent at least three minutes of her precious hour staring at her battered running shoes, her mind an utter blank.

"Time's a wastin'," Daniel finally drawled. "Where do we go first, ma'am?"

"Oh . . . oh, anywhere," she said, awakening from her fugue. "The lighthouse, I guess." She pointed south, to the structure a thousand feet away. Putting the camera around her neck, she then picked up the hamper Mark had deposited at her feet.

"Here, get out the rest of your equipment and I'll put this thing in my trunk until lunchtime."

Realizing that it was foolish to haul the heavy basket around, Lorelei quickly extracted her voice-activated recorder and binoculars from the hamper, before turning the basket over to Daniel.

He stole a peek inside. "This is a pretty serious lunch you've packed for us, sweetheart. Glad to see that you really know how to feed a guy."

"Not according to Howard, I didn't," she muttered, and then ducked her head in confusion at the arrested look on Daniel's face. Why in the world had she said something as stupid as that? she wondered, squeezing her eyes shut.

But when warm lips softly caressed her cheek, Lorelei's lids flew open. She moved a hasty step away from the temptation of finding comfort in Daniel's strong arms. It could become a habit she might not be able to break.

As Lorelei retreated from his touch, Daniel took a ragged breath and then turned to store the hamper in the car's trunk. He had wanted to hug her and rock away her pain. But since she wasn't ready to accept that from him, he decided to give her a minute to compose herself.

That s.o.b. ex-husband of hers had a lot to answer for, he fumed. Maybe he would look up the fool and send Dr. Howard Taylor to some other plastic surgeon, sporting a nose that needed major reconstruction.

Picking up his sketching pad and pencils, Daniel strode over to where Lorelei stood, looking up at the nearby lighthouse.

"The small size of the building always surprises me," she said conversationally when she heard Daniel approach. Happy that her voice was under control, she started walking toward the whitewashed brick structure.

"It looks like a Midwestern farmhouse," Daniel commented offhandedly, taking his cue from Lorelei's manner. "Although I've never seen one with a huge tower sticking out of its roof. Is the light still in use?"

"No, the coast guard shut it down because the light was obscured by fog too many days of the year. They built another one nearly at sea level on the very tip of the peninsula. We'll go down that way in a bit. I want to check out the plants around the tidal pools over there."

By the time they reached the lighthouse, Lorelei had donned her professional mantle and examined the landscaping around the lighthouse with a critical eye. The plantings made a strong contribution to the atmosphere around the nineteenth-century structure.

"Dan, could you make a quick drawing of the lighthouse and include the twisted junipers flanking either side of the entrance?"

"No problem," he said, flipping open his sketchbook and sharpening a soft drawing pencil.

While Daniel did the illustration, Lorelei took a few snapshots of the flowers in the area, speaking into her recorder with a verbal shorthand that would trip her memory when she transcribed the tape later.

When she finished a few minutes later, she was surprised that Daniel had already completed his drawing. "Can I see it now?" she asked softly, not sure of how he felt about showing anyone his sketches before final polishing.

But Daniel just handed her the pad with a smile. And when Lorelei opened to the first page, she realized that there was nothing raw about the well-crafted picture . . . except for the starkness of the whitewashed building, which he had captured standing strong and resolute against the clean morning sky.

"This is wonderful! Look how you put in the feel of the constant wind." She pointed to the image of the bent and twisted evergreens. Gazing up at Daniel, Lorelei didn't even try to hide the admiration she felt for his expertise.

"Thanks, Lori. If you'd take photos of all the plants I work on today, I'll have really polished illustrations for you in the next week or two. Wish I had time to do a whole series of line drawings of the lighthouse. That building just radiates a sense of history. And I'll bet the aura is even more powerful inside." Daniel tried to keep from looking longingly at the entrance of the structure. "But I guess we have an appointment to keep with those tidal pools you mentioned."

Lorelei could see the architect's compulsion to examine old buildings in Daniel's gold-green irises. However, she decided to tease *him* a little, for a change.

"Yes, there're guided tours down to the pools leaving from the visitor's center. But I think it would be better if we went by ourselves and examined the area at our own pace. We can drive over."

"Yeah, sure," Daniel agreed resignedly to her pronouncement. He flipped his pad closed, and with one more glance behind him, turned in the direction of the parking lot.

"Of course, if you're really interested, we *could* spend a few minutes inside the lighthouse."

Whipping around, Daniel saw the devil lighting Lorelei's blue eyes. "Why you sadistic little witch!" he exclaimed pleasantly, shaking a finger at her.

Laughing, Lorelei let Daniel take her arm and tug her up the short staircase to the building's front door.

Inside, she pointed out the living areas on the first floor, which were furnished with nineteenth-century period pieces. "I know what you mean about a sense of history captured here. Every time I go through these rooms, I feel like the lighthouse keeper and his family have just stepped out."

As they wandered around, she watched his reaction to the surprisingly spacious rooms. His delight made her glad that they were playing tourist for a few minutes.

At the thought of tourists, she looked around for the hordes that usually came through the building. But they were all alone. Maybe Tuesday mornings were a slack time.

Their examination of the lower level ended at the base of the staircase leading up to the light tower.

"You should go topside," Lorelei advised Daniel. "There's something up there that a resident of Los Angeles doesn't get to experience from one year to the next."

"And what might that be?" Daniel asked, although he thought he knew what her punchline was.

"A smogless view of the horizon," she replied, fulfilling his prediction.

"Well then, let's go, go, go," Daniel said, giving her backside several little pats to get her moving.

And move she did. With the sensual feel of his long fingers warming her sensitive skin, even through the denim of her jeans, Lorelei led the way to the top with binoculars and camera bouncing on their straps.

Feeling as if a dangerous demon were in pursuit, she didn't even stop to glance at the two curved bedrooms ingeniously tucked into the tower walls.

At the apex of the stairs, the blood pounded so loudly in her ears that Lorelei couldn't hear if Daniel was still behind her, or if the architect's soul couldn't resist the pull of those clever little bedrooms.

But he was right there, stepping up to her level when she paused to regain her breath. She was panting hard enough as it was, so she purposefully averted her eyes from his gorgeous face to focus on the whorled pattern the steps made below them.

Now, doesn't that staircase look like the inside of a chambered nautilus? she wondered. *How did that poem go?*

" 'Build thee more stately mansions, o my soul . . .' " Daniel quoted quietly into her ear. And Lorelei suddenly gripped the banister, not knowing if her knees had caved in because of the quick climb, or if it was because he quoted the opening line to the Oliver Wendel Holmes poem she searched for in her mind.

"Steady there, honey. Let me take some of your stuff and hold my hand. Can't have our favorite author tumbling down the stairs before she's finished with her research."

Daniel's gentle teasing helped Lorelei steady herself. But she didn't refuse his offer to carry her recorder when she climbed the ladder that scaled the final distance to the open-air promenade.

Guarded by shoulder-high, wrought-iron fencing, the catwalk circled the outside of the glassed-in room that held the lighthouse's beveled Fresnel lens.

Taking several deep breaths in the gusting air, Lorelei finally felt the world right itself again. She looked around, once more surprised that there were no tourists up here, like there had been every other time she visited the lighthouse.

Realizing that Daniel still held her hand, she tugged her fingers out of his firm grip. "Thanks, Dan. I'm all right now," she said, using her freed hand to indicate the ocean view. "And this is what I wanted you to see."

"Magnificent," Daniel murmured, walking to the guard rail and looking to the west and the surging sea.

"If you ever get a chance to come back here in winter, you can see the migration of gray whales up from the Baja California peninsula," Lorelei said, joining him at the railing. "That glassed-in building to the south is the Whale Overlook. It shelters viewers from the winter wind."

"Oh, we'll be sure to come back and see the whales," Daniel promised, turning to look meaningfully into Lorelei's eyes.

"And to the north," she said, hurriedly moving a few steps clockwise, "are the naval installations. Somewhere in those buildings is the Anti-submarine Warfare School where my dad taught just before he retired."

"I remember somebody saying at the picnic that he was a sub commander. Did he captain one of the big nuclear boats?"

"No," Lorelei laughed, "he hates them, calls them underwater resort hotels. 'Give me bulkheads that I can see curve and walkways that don't have room for a combine harvester,' he always says."

Daniel chuckled, and Lorelei had to stop herself from gaping at the glorious sight of that smile, combined with the beauty of his dark red hair whipping in the wind. Almost as if someone else were controlling her movements, Lorelei lifted Mark's camera and snapped off several quick shots of Daniel.

Hopefully, one of them would turn out. It would be something to remember him by after this assignment was over. Forcefully turning away from one of nature's better designs, she walked to the northeast.

"There's North Island. The section nearest to us is the U.S. Naval Air Station, and the city of Coronado takes up the rest of the area. That's where my folks live and I grew up."

"Coronado? Hey, isn't that the Hotel Ramona?" Daniel said. He reached over and commandeered Lorelei's binoculars, forcing her to rest her cheek against his while he examined the image magnified by the lenses. "Take a picture of the place, Lori. I see a certain cozy bench on the cliff over there that I never want to forget. It's where I first necked with my future wife."

Damn it, Daniel wasn't playing fair! Grabbing the binoculars out of his hand, she moved back to glare up at his grinning face.

"This camera doesn't have a telephoto lens," she informed him. Lord, why couldn't he take her "no" to his proposal seriously? She knew her own mind, and she would not marry him. The only thing was, she was having trouble convincing her heart, body, and her heated blood that she knew what was best for all of them.

"Gee, that's too bad," Daniel said, almost as if he had heard her troubled thoughts. "You know, Lori, there's one thing I don't understand. If you lived in Coronado so long, why didn't you ever visit the Hotel Ramona before last Saturday?"

"Oh, I don't know," she said. "I almost went there a dozen times, but something always seemed to come up at the last minute, and I didn't go. I guess it *is* sort of strange when you think about it."

"Maybe fate had some sort of secret plan," Daniel suggested.

"Fate? What are you talking about?" she demanded.

"I don't know," he retorted. "Who am I to understand the workings of kismet?" He shrugged. But then he decided it was time for him to give that potent force a little practical help. Abruptly placing the recorder on the ground, he reached over to take Mark's camera out of her hands and add it to the pile.

Ignoring Lorelei's squeak of surprised protest, he deftly moved her binoculars out of the way, just before capturing her face between his hands and fiercely covering her mouth with his. Gratified when her lips automatically softened in response to his questing tongue, Daniel used his body to push her gently back against the glass wall surrounding the light housing.

Somewhere in a deep recess of her mind, Lorelei knew that she should be protesting Daniel's sensual onslaught. *They were out in broad daylight, for heaven's sakes!* But the rest of her body told her brain to shut up.

Finally giving in to her need for him, Lorelei fully welcomed the honey-sweet probe of Daniel's tongue, and responded to the intimate press of his strong thighs. Wrapping her arms tightly around his waist, she felt the progression of his arousal. And with each hard, lengthening pulse, Lorelei experienced a thrilling jolt of pleasure that ran from the apex of her femininity to the very ends of her fingers.

Sensing her complete surrender, Daniel settled his hand lower on Lorelei's back, urging her into even closer contact. But within seconds, he knew that he was a hair's-breadth away from completely losing control.

He tried to ease away from the warm cradle of Lorelei's hips. But her body followed his, delightfully rubbing against his most blatant claim to masculinity.

Daniel had no doubt that, in another minute, he and Lorelei would have figured out how to make love *al fresco* and on their feet. But the sudden echoing ring of high-pitched voices reverberating up the staircase alerted him to the fact that they were no longer alone with the wind and the sky and the sea.

As it was, he had just managed to pull away from Lorelei and look through the glass panes of the light housing when he saw three little girls and their parents bubble out onto the catwalk. Taking Lorelei's hand, he tugged her along until they were a full half-circle away from the chattering family.

Confused by the sudden loss of Daniel's warmth, Lorelei looked around in a haze of frustrated desire. But then her eyes regained the power to focus, and she suddenly saw that the tourist season had finally come back to Point Loma.

Lorelei almost moaned out loud when she realized how close she had come to making love with Daniel in plain sight of greater San Diego! Wishing that she could somehow become invisible, she yanked her hand out of his and quietly circled behind the family, who, thankfully, were engrossed in looking out over the railing at the ocean.

With the power of adrenaline racing in her blood, she was through the exit door before the newcomers could have seen more than a blue jean-clad streak. Down the ladder and staircase she flew, with her Nikes barely touching the steps.

Pushing out of the lighthouse door, she ran the whole thousand feet to the parking lot, stopping only when she reached Daniel's Corvette. Bending over, she lay her head on the low roof, coughing and choking while she forced air into her starving lungs. When she finally caught her breath, Lorelei raised her head, searching the path for some sign of Daniel.

She wanted to tell him that this research trip had been a complete fiasco and that he was fired.

But he didn't appear. When five and ten minutes went by, Lorelei finally thought to look up at the lighthouse tower. Squinting in the bright sunlight, she suddenly realized that Daniel was still on the catwalk, and he was surrounded by the three little girls and their parents.

Lifting the binoculars that somehow had remained around her neck through the whole upsetting episode, Lorelei focused on the scene, trying to figure out just what was happening. After a minute, Daniel's situation became clear.

For the next few minutes, a stream of giggles bubbled from her lips every time her mind replayed the scene she had observed on the tower. If she lived to be a hundred, she would always remember the picture of Daniel holding the youngest child in his arms, while the other two girls clung to his side. And completing the tableau were the children's parents, pointing to various objects in the distance. They were probably showing Daniel all the places of interest Lorelei had failed to identify for him.

Leave it to Daniel to come up smelling roses, even in the most embarrassing situation, Lorelei thought with another chuckle. It seemed that not sixty seconds after he had lost one tour guide, he had found five devoted replacements.

TEN

"Shame on you, Lorelei, deserting me like that." Daniel plopped her recorder and sample case on her lap, before throwing himself on the ground beside her. He leaned his back against the car door.

"Me, ashamed? Me!" Lorelei protested loudly, but she was unable to keep the amusement she still felt out of her voice. "I'm not the person who almost got us arrested for indecent behavior in a public place. I'm surprised those people up there didn't hand you over to the ranger."

"Oh, they were too sorry for me to do that."

"Sorry for you?"

"Yeah, somehow, they got the idea that my bride and I had just had our first quarrel . . . over whether we should go deep sea fishing or shopping."

"Oh, Dan, Dan, you missed your calling. Forget architecture. It looks like you're much more suited to fiction writing."

"Touché!" he said, chuckling. Happy that Lorelei was still talking to him after he had put her in such a compromising situation, Daniel leaned over to drop a light kiss on her cheek.

Immediately jumping to her feet, Lorelei fought the desire to touch the tingling spot on her skin. "No more of that stuff, buddy," she cautioned. "It's what got us into trouble in the first place. Come on, Dan, time to earn our money. Let's get back on schedule and drive over to the tidal pools."

The instant the words left her mouth, Lorelei realized that her laughing fit must have neutralized the self-directed anger she had felt about losing control with Daniel. So instead of firing him as she had planned, she just waited for him to unlock the passenger door.

When they reached the tip of the peninsula, Daniel parked the car a few feet from the edge of the cliffs. Outside the vehicle, they stood for a minute, looking down at the sedimentary rock that had been cut into natural steps by the wind and wave action of winter storms.

"Where do we begin, Lori?" Daniel asked.

Begin? Confused, Lorelei searched his face for illumination. She didn't see how there could be *any* beginning for them. If only they had met in a few years. Five or six years in the future, Daniel would be a practicing architect, and she would have a degree or two in ornamental horticulture. Both of them would still be young enough to make a life together, to have the family Daniel wanted so much . . . that she wanted so much.

"Lori, are you all right?" His fingers brushed her cheek, jolting Lorelei out of the wonderful alternate universe in which she had been wandering.

"Of course, I'm all right," she said, more tartly than she should have. "But why are we just standing here? Don't you realize how much we have to get done?"

"Yes, I do. That's why I asked a minute ago where

you wanted us to begin work," Daniel countered in a soft, patient voice.

"Oh, God. I'm sorry for snapping, Dan. Just let me get my things, and then we can find a way down. I want to examine the flower species growing near the water."

"Do you want me to take the food hamper with us now, or wait until later?" Daniel asked.

Lorelei looked at the twenty- or thirty-foot drop to the bottom of the cliff and then at her watch. "I can't believe it's almost eleven thirty! If you don't mind, I'd rather get a good start before we break for lunch, but there's no use having to trudge back up here for the basket later. Can you manage? I have my stuff . . ."

"There's something to be said for traveling light." Daniel laughed, putting his sketch pad into the hamper and lifting it high on his shoulder.

"Let's put the lunch here where it won't get wet," she suggested when they reached the area above the high watermark.

It was low tide, and the spring deposits of sand had already formed enough of a beach for them to negotiate the lower ramparts of the jutting cliffs. Lorelei knew that during the winter the sand disappeared, and it was impossible to reach the area on foot.

At first glance, the place seemed devoid of plants. But Lorelei finally found a thick growth of pink ice plant, and then she spotted a stand of tangerine-colored California poppies in the distance through her binoculars.

"Dan, I don't know if it would be worthwhile for you to do a sketch of the ice plant," Lori said. "I'd like to show how the leaves actually sparkle. But I don't think you can do that with only your drawing pencil."

"No, however, I can make a few written notations, and then re-do the drawing in watercolors later."

"But how will you remember the exact shades?" she wondered.

"I have a pretty good memory for color. It's sort of like being a musician with perfect pitch . . . just a genetic fluke, I guess. One of the things that I'll probably pass on to my children," he quietly mused.

"Well, g-go ahead then, do a d-drawing," Lorelei stuttered. Why did he have to remind her of all the glorious attributes he had to offer his future children? She imagined that the boys would get broad shoulders and long, strong legs. And maybe the girls would have gold-green eyes and strawberry-blond hair.

Strawberry blond? Lorelei pondered for a second. No, the red in Daniel's thick mane was too dark. Only if he married a very fair woman would their children . . . Oh for heaven's sake, why did she keep running off like this into fantasy?

"There are many kinds of ice plant growing at will on the California Coast," Lorelei said forcefully into her recorder, trying to refocus on the purpose of this expedition. "The group got its name because of the tiny transparent blisters found on the thick leaves. They glisten like ice in the sun. The flower has been planted or naturalized along the coast of California, from the border with Mexico to the Monterey peninsula.

"Although it's also used on the verges of the superhighways, it is best adapted for the wind and salty air near the beach. It is a tough and forgiving plant, found in a variety of brilliant colors."

Lorelei hit the off button. Daniel looked up from the drawing he was doing, his expression thoughtful. "You really have all that information at your fingertips, don't you?"

"Oh, this is pretty basic stuff. Any serious gardener has a vast store of knowledge on a wide range of plants. The really hard part for me is knowing what to do in the greenhouses . . . how to prepare just the right soil mixtures and how to protect the spores and seedlings from damping-off diseases. Some of it's experience, but a lot of it requires research and true experimentation.

"Tom Sumoto and I are working out a whole range of techniques to protect our plants . . . the more natural, the better. We try to do things in a way that doesn't hurt us, the customer, or the environment. That's why I'm going to the university fulltime this fall. I want access to the latest knowledge and to keep on the cutting edge of research."

"We think alike about learning, Lori," Daniel said seriously. "It has to be a life-long pursuit. And although I know you're already a fine horticulturist, I can see you taking classes even after you've got all the degrees you want. There we'll be, fifty years from now, still trying to keep up, and taking classes with a bunch of young whippersnappers."

Lorelei laughed in delight. Yes, Daniel really understood her drive to get a formal education. And well he should, she wryly reminded herself, it would take several years for *him* to complete the journey to his own degrees.

Shaking her head, she tried to derail her train of thought. All this was detracting from her work.

"Well, let's find us a few tidepools," she said forcefully.

"You mean it ain't lunchtime yet?" Daniel complained.

"I'll compromise . . . just one tidepool and then we can eat," Lorelei said.

Amid grumblings, both vocal and gastral, the two trudged a bit further north, until they found a deep pocket that had been scoured out of flat sandstone.

Lorelei peered into the miniature aquarium, entranced

by the busy little crabs, and by the tiny flower-like anemones that were stuck to the sheltered sides of the pool.

"I can't resist including the anemones, though they're actually animals," she said.

"Animals?" Daniel dipped his finger into the shallow water, intent on investigating one of the waving, petal-like arms.

"No! Don't touch!" Lorelei shouted.

Daniel jerked back, and then looked at her, a half smile on his mouth.

"I wasn't pulling your leg," Lorelei responded to the suspicion dancing in his eyes. "Those pretty petals really are tentacles, and they have stinging cells that can paralyze fish and give humans a nasty reaction. I don't think a sting is fatal, but it's painful enough."

"Well, thanks for the warning. Since I'm already dying from hunger, I don't think I'd like to add another irritant to the load."

"All right, all right," Lorelei laughed. "Never let it be said that I was cruel to anyone. Let's go back to the basket and save you from fainting away."

"This is terrific chicken," Daniel said a few minutes later, having devoured two pieces of the tasty meat. "I bet even the Colonel would like to find out just what herbs and spices *you* use to get this flavor."

"Thank you, thank you. It's a variation on my grandmother's recipe that I came up with a few years ago."

"Lori . . . Lorelei, I'll bet in spite of what you said this morning that chicken isn't the only thing you're good at cooking. Please don't get mad at me, honey, but isn't it time you realized that your ex-husband tried to cover up his own problems by doing a number on your self-confidence?"

Hearing the depth of caring in Daniel's voice, Lorelei responded with utter honesty. "Of course, you're right.

That comment just popped out of my subconscious this morning. Most of the time I understand that Howard has a real flaw in his make-up. I've thought about it a lot; maybe it's because his father was killed when he was so young. Howard seemed to feel that the world owed him everything he wanted . . . instantly.''

"Like a baby thinking that everybody exists just to take care of him," Daniel interpreted.

"Exactly. I used to make all sorts of excuses for his selfish behavior. But after meeting you, I see how foolish that was.''

"What do you mean, after meeting me?" Daniel asked, putting his third piece of chicken on the plate.

"I mean that *you* had even more cause to be angry at the world. You didn't have a father—or a mother—and look how far you've come on your own!"

"Oh, don't go making me into some sort of hero, Lorelei," Daniel said uncomfortably. "I haven't always been able to look at things very objectively. Like you, I found it hard to maintain my self-esteem after being discarded so casually. For years, I thought that there must have been something horribly wrong with me for my mother to stuff me into that trashcan.''

"Oh, Daniel, that's something I'll never be able to understand, either. The only thing I know is that *you* had absolutely nothing to do with your mother acting in such an insane way.''

"And I'm equally sure that Howard Taylor must be certifiably crazy to have left you for any other woman.''

Lorelei looked down at the plate of food in her lap, realizing that she hadn't even taken a bite of the chicken. She made a determined effort to eat something, but found it hard to get the food past the lump in her throat.

She reached into the hamper for two cans of soda. Giving one to Daniel, she popped the tab on hers and took a big gulp.

"Sometimes it's hard to swallow the hand that fate deals us, isn't it, sweetheart?" Daniel lifted his own soda can in an ironic salute to his mixed metaphor.

"We can but try to make lemonade with the lemons," Lorelei countered with one of her own. But then she got up enough courage to ask Daniel a question that had been bothering her.

"Dan, have you ever tried to find out about your mother . . . or your father? To find out what really happened?"

"Ah, Lorelei, don't you know that it's every orphan's dream to discover that he was kidnapped from desperate parents who have turned the world upside-down in the search for their beloved child. I alternated between that fantasy and one in which I became a millionaire by the time I was eighteen.

"In that scenario, my mother appears one day, begging me on her knees for forgiveness. I just turn my back on her, after providing the money she needs to get a vital operation, of course." He laughed wryly.

"Oh, Dan," was all Lorelei could say to that honest revelation.

"Actually, I did try to find my missing folks. But remember, I wasn't placed for adoption. I was totally abandoned. I went to the police just before I left St. Louis, and they tried to help. They even gave me a copy of the original report. But there was nothing in it, except for the time of day, and the name of the street where I was found . . . wrapped in newspaper, with absolutely nothing to identify me."

Lorelei impulsively leaned over to kiss Daniel on the cheek. "Well, here's to us survivors. Two wonderful people with a hell of a lot going for them!"

"Here, here!" Daniel agreed, raising his can of soda in a toast.

Feeling at peace with themselves, and each other, Lorelei and Daniel tackled the food with gusto. After carefully stowing all their trash in the basket, they went back to work with renewed purpose.

By three, Lorelei was satisfied that they had located everything she could use at Point Loma.

"We might as well get going, there wasn't as much as I had hoped for here, but I'm really satisfied with what we've gotten. Quality, if not quantity. Thanks, Dan. You did a great job."

ELEVEN

It was after five when Daniel finally pulled to a stop in front of Lorelei's building. He looked over at her and realized that she must have fallen asleep in the last few minutes.

Daniel thought she looked like a teenager, sitting there with one leg tucked under her, that long ponytail trailing over one shoulder. There was a soft vulnerability about the way she slept, her head turned toward him, her hand resting just a hair's-breadth away from his thigh.

His body automatically tightened at the memory of how her fingers had stroked him on his thighs, and everywhere else. It was all he could do to keep himself from spiriting her upstairs to that wide, old-fashioned bed. He wanted to watch her awaken to his touch and give him the warm, moist welcome he remembered from Sunday.

But he knew that he might lose all the gains he had made with her today if he gave in to that desire. He was sure she loved him as much as he loved her. But Lorelei was still holding out on him.

There was something she was terrified of. Something

that was making her fight so hard against committing herself to him. He had to figure out what it was. Now that he had found her, he wasn't about to lose his Lorelei.

With that settled in his mind, Daniel reached over to shake Lorelei awake gently.

"Honey . . . Lori, come on sleepyhead, we're here."

"What? Oh, I wasn't sleeping, Daniel. Just resting my eyes," she protested, and then gave a prodigious yawn to belie her words. Still a bit disoriented, she looked out at the empty parking lot in confusion. "Julie must have closed up. Is it after five already?"

"Yep, nearly half past," Daniel confirmed.

"Maybe I did sleep just a bit," Lorelei admitted sheepishly. "Well, let's get my stuff."

She opened her door, and waited while Daniel removed her basket from the trunk. They walked up the stairs to her apartment and Daniel deposited the hamper just inside the living room when she opened the door.

"Would you like to stay for supper, Dan? I know my stomach is telling me that lunch was a long time ago."

"Much as I'd like to, Susan and John are expecting me." Daniel was very proud that he hadn't even hesitated. "You told Mark that we were going to the Zoo tomorrow, and to be here at eight thirty, didn't you?"

Not really understanding Daniel's surprising change of attitude, Lorelei could only nod mutely in confirmation.

"Then, I'll be here at eight twenty-five for my good morning kiss," Daniel promised.

Not daring to even give her a good-night kiss, he turned and ambled down the stairs, two at a time.

Lorelei just stared after him in dismay. What was going on here? Daniel had pursued her like mad all day long. But now, just when she was thinking that things might work out for them, he went off to spend the night with the Grants! And he didn't even ask if she wanted to come along for dinner.

Would she ever understand the man? And did it matter?

Maybe it was best if she called off tomorrow's trip and sent back the book advance to George Tolliver. It seemed that there was no way she would ever finish this project with her sanity intact.

With her temper rising, Lorelei marched over to the phone. It would take Daniel half an hour to get to her sister's house, but Mark might be home from the office. And even if he wasn't, she could leave him a message on his recorder.

But he answered on the second ring.

"Have the lawyers dismantled their microscopes?" she asked by way of a greeting.

"Lori? I was just going to call you. No, everything is still a mess. I thought we had the sucker tied up in a neat package an hour ago, and then those damned weasels dug up another objection out of left field. Honey, it looks like I'll have to miss the Zoo, too.

"So, tell me," Mark went on without giving her a chance to break in, "how did you make out with our favorite redhead?"

Lorelei knew he didn't mean anything by the double entendre buried in his words. But her cheeks still flushed rosy-red, remembering just how she had "made out" with Daniel at the top of the Point Loma lighthouse.

"Oh, I got everything I wanted," she replied, biting her wayward tongue when she came up with an ambiguous response of her own. "I mean, Daniel did some really fine drawings."

"Look, Lori, while I'm sure I could have helped you with some damned good photos, I really don't know when I'll be free, and I don't want to hold you back. Would you hate me a lot if I backed out of the project altogether?"

"Mark, I understand, and I wouldn't even hate you a little."

"Great. Say, how about being my date for the contract-signing party that's scheduled two weeks from Friday? I'm sure the lawyers will have everything squared away by then."

"I can't give you a firm answer until I check my calendar downstairs. And right now, I'm too tired from all that sea air to see straight."

"OK, Lori. I'll be in touch. You get some rest."

With that directive, he hung up.

"Well, that's one down," Lorelei muttered to herself. She dialed Susan's house a few minutes later, only to get a busy signal. The same annoying tone greeted her next five attempts.

Sighing, she finally obeyed her grumbling stomach and heated up leftovers for dinner. Eating in front of the television, she watched a rerun of *Aliens* on the cable channel.

Maybe she should take some pointers from the heroine. Now *there* was a lady who knew how to hold her own against any foe . . . slimy business executives, gung-ho space marines . . . and a monster who was the ultimate extraterrestrial single mother.

Lorelei tried her sister one more time before falling into her bed. With a teenager in the house, she thought after getting another busy signal, her sister really should get the telephone company's call waiting option.

It was one of those days. Lorelei woke up with a slight sore throat, and then the glass she used to gargle with saltwater shattered all over the bathroom floor. After barely avoiding a sliced foot as she cleaned up the mess, she dressed for the trip to the Zoo.

Sometime during the night, Lorelei had awakened and realized that if she scuttled the *Blooming San Diego* project, she would only be hurting herself. The plain truth was that she needed the money.

The advance would pay her current expenses, and any royalties down the road would help keep her in school. She had also admitted to herself at three in the morning that Daniel Logan was a damned fine artist. And she was sure his drawings would help her book sales much more than any pictures she could come up with. With that thought in mind, Lorelei pulled on her clothes, and waited for Daniel to arrive.

"Looks like it's started to rain," Daniel offered brightly as the door swung open.

"Good old Murphy's Law," Lorelei muttered when she saw the first fat drops plop on the ground.

Oh, oh! Daniel thought to himself when he saw the look on her face. Better not even try for a kiss this morning. Maybe he had made a serious tactical error by not staying for dinner last night.

"Does that L.A. prima dona handle well in the rain?" Lorelei asked, pointing to Daniel's Corvette.

"I don't really know. Come to think of it, we haven't had any rain since I got it," Daniel admitted.

"Then I'll drive. We don't have to wait for Mark. He's bowed out because of business problems," Lorelei announced, ignoring the big grin that news provoked. After locating a waterproof carry-all for her equipment, she marched over to the ancient Nova.

The rain arrived in torrents the minute she pulled the car onto the freeway. The half-hour journey to the Zoo turned into an hour and forty-five minute nightmare, while San Diego residents tried to remember their wet-weather driving skills.

It was still pouring as they neared the exit ramp for Balboa Park, where the Zoo was located.

"Well, it looks like this will go on all day. I'm afraid

we'll have to turn back," Lorelei said, turning her windshield wipers to the fastest setting.

"Isn't there any place around here with a roof and plants that you want to include?" Daniel asked, hoping he could find out what was bugging Lorelei before she dismissed him altogether.

"There is the botanical building near the art museum," she remembered. "The conservatory has a wonderful collection of bromiliads and epiphites that I should reference in the book. But it's got a lath roof, and it might be too wet inside to do any work."

"Well, let's try anyway," Daniel said decisively.

As luck would have it, the rain stopped just as Lorelei pulled into the parking lot between the botanical building and the museum.

"Fantastic!" Daniel murmured when they entered the domed center section of the building. His architect's eye was first attracted to the high, lath-worked roof. But then the green impact of hundreds of flower-studded plants made him turn to Lorelei. "You're going to have a field day in here, honey."

Lorelei couldn't help returning his infectious smile. She didn't seem to have any defenses where Daniel was concerned. And to be honest with herself, she was close to admitting that she didn't care anymore.

Slipping her hand through the arm Daniel offered her, she walked along with him, working out a plan of action that would make some sense of the lush profusion of ruby-throated bromiliads and delicately painted orchids.

"Why don't you take shots of the plants you want illustrated?" Daniel suggested. "Then I'll make some quick color and size notes on them. And if we have time, I'll do a few sketches of the really unique flowers."

"That's very logical, Daniel. But even if you're just

taking notes, I don't see how you'll keep up with me and know which plants I've photographed."

"Hmmm, that is a problem. Hey, I've got it!" Daniel opened his sketch pad and tore out a few blank sheets. "Let's rip this paper into thin strips and you can put them on the plants you want me to make notes on. And maybe we better tell the guards what we're doing, so they don't get excited."

The plan worked. Lorelei was free to go at her own pace, and Daniel was able to take the time he needed to make sketches and meaningful notations that he could coordinate with Lorelei's photographs when he did the final drawings.

They toiled all through the morning, not even stopping for lunch. Lorelei was in a horticulturist's heaven, but she finally had to quit when it started raining again.

She located Daniel, who had just closed up his thick sketch book and was trying to protect it by putting the pad under his shirt.

"Let's call it a day and find some place to buy lunch," she suggested as she placed her equipment in her water-proof carry-all. "Why don't you put your sketch book in here, Dan?"

"Sure enough," he agreed, handing it to her. But some-how, in the transfer, the bound sheath of paper slipped out of Lorelei's hand. With reflexes that even surprised herself, she managed to catch the sketch book before it reached the ground.

"Whew," she breathed. "Close call." Starting to close up the pad, which had flipped open, one of the pages caught her eye. A very strange plant indeed, she thought, looking at the image Daniel must have captured of her sometime during the long morning's work.

She examined the soft, romantic curves he had used to capture her in three-quarter profile. Surely she didn't look like that. So serene, so wise . . . so lovely. Gazing up at Daniel's suddenly guarded face, Lorelei realized that she was too touched to speak. She also found herself wishing that she could draw.

She'd love to present Daniel with a sketch that caught not only his masculine beauty and razor-sharp intelligence, but also reflected the kind and gentle soul that seemed to shine out of his hazel eyes.

Carefully closing the sketch book, Lorelei gave it a place of honor in her carry-all.

TWELVE

With the rain coming down even harder, Lorelei and Daniel sprinted out of the botanical building toward the parking lot.

"I can't even see the car," Daniel yelled in the rising wind. "Let's take shelter over there." He pointed to the structure a dozen yards to their right.

Without waiting for Lorelei's agreement, he took her arm and pulled her under the eaves of the small house, incongruously set on a little patch of grass in the middle of the parking lot.

"This is strange," Lorelei said as they reached the protection of the building's overhang. "I've got a lifetime membership to the museum and come here all the time, so I know this place wasn't here six weeks ago."

"No," Daniel agreed, pointing to a large information sign. "That's because it was just built. And talk about the forces of fate! I am now a true believer." He grabbed Lorelei by the shoulders in excitement.

"Do you know what this is? Frank Lloyd Wright's Unisonian Automatic House."

Feeling as bemused as Daniel looked, Lorelei peeked around his broad body to read the salient points on the information sign for herself.

It seemed that this full-scale, walk-through model was the only Wright house ever constructed in San Diego. It would grace the parking lot for several months, and then the building would be broken down and shipped to Taliesin West, the architectural school Wright had founded in Scottsdale, Arizona.

"I've been thinking of doing advanced work at the school," Daniel said, as she read the last line. "That's what I meant by fate. This is almost like a portent that I should apply. I only wish I had been born fifty years sooner and could have studied directly with *The Man*."

Lorelei smiled when she heard the capital letters in his voice. "Well, disciple, why don't we go inside and see what your master has wrought?" she suggested, capturing Daniel's hand and pulling him to the entrance.

The guard at the door checked Lorelei's art museum membership card and took one of the guest passes that came with it, for Daniel's admission.

"You've got the place to yourselves this afternoon. Looks like everyone else was afraid they were going to melt in that rare stuff out there," the man said with a laugh. "You can walk through at will, just don't touch any of the furniture or decorations."

"We'll be good," Daniel promised.

Once inside, his head constantly swiveled as he tried to catch every detail and fix it in his memory. Remembering the guard's warning, Daniel had to fight not to run his fingers over the hand-thrown pottery on the end tables, or to rub the nubby-textured cloth covering the couches. He finally shoved both hands deep into his pants pockets.

"Destruction of the Box," he murmured under his

breath, as he stood in the center of the light-filled living room, rocking back and forth from toe to heel.

"What does that mean, Dan?" Lorelei asked.

"It's the concept of opening up the four walls of the ordinary house, Lori." His hands escaped his pockets to grab her arm and lead her around the area. "Wright believed in letting the outside environment into a structure, by reducing interior walls and using corner windows and skylights."

Daniel's hand made a sweep of the place. "And the beauty of this design is that each family can rearrange the room dividers according to their own needs. And even if you built dozens of these in a tract, each house could be unique."

"What a wonderful idea," Lorelei said, looking around again. She realized that, in this particular arrangement, the living area was designed for entertainment. Lighted by large windows in the ten-foot-high walls, the room contained a massive fireplace, conversational centers . . . and a baby grand piano.

Of course, that meant there were only two small bedrooms, she noticed, when they walked down a long hallway and looked inside the sleeping quarters. But with the built-in furniture Wright had designed, nothing seemed cramped or cluttered.

While they wandered the house, rain continued to drum on the flat roof with unseasonable intensity. But Lorelei felt warm and snug when Daniel slipped his arm around her waist and held her to his side as they marveled at the state-of-the-art kitchen.

When they had finally seen everything, the pair went back to the living room. Standing by the tall glass doors that led out to a small patio, Daniel let out a big sigh.

"Well, I think we'd better go. Either that, or I'll be

tempted to hide in here and become a permanent part of the exhibit.''

He deepened his voice dramatically. "And that's how it happened, folks. He is doomed to sleep the day away, hanging in the closet, and then wander the halls during the hours of the night.''

Lorelei laughed as Daniel swirled an imaginary cape in front of his face to become a modern-day Dracula.

"Well, to save you from becoming one of the undead, how about joining me for lunch somewhere? I'm afraid my favorite place here, the outdoor café, is a washout,'' she said, turning an ear to the sound of the unremitting rain. "But we can find something just outside the park.''

"I have a better idea,'' Daniel countered. "How about if we stop at a grocery and I get the makings of my famous kitchen-sink omelette?''

"Don't tell me that you're also a gourmet cook,'' Lorelei groaned.

"Oh, I'd never tell you that,'' Daniel said, reaching over to tuck a damp strand of hair behind her ear.

The gentle show of affection brought a lump to her throat. She suddenly realized that every time they had been together, Daniel seemed to need the simple act of touching her. And intuitively, Lorelei understood. A boy growing up in an orphanage might get enough to eat and a place to sleep, but there would be no mother to hug him in the morning or give him a good-night kiss. There would be no father to ruffle his hair and tell him how proud he was to have him for a son.

She impulsively wrapped her arms around his waist, knowing that, in spite of his deprived childhood, he had grown into a strong, wonderfully mature man. But as she buried her face on his wide shoulder, Lorelei still wished that she somehow could give Daniel every bit of love he had missed as a child.

"I love you, I love you," Daniel repeated in her ear. "And I am always going to love you."

With that soft declaration a warm wave of peace settled over Lorelei. All of a sudden, nothing mattered to her any more, but the facts that Daniel loved her and she loved him. So what if he needed two or three years to finish his degree? So what if a long apprenticeship faced him after that? It would work out, somehow. Tears of relief began rolling down her cheeks, and she couldn't seem to stem the flow.

Oh lord, Daniel agonized, I didn't mean to scare her. Please let her understand how much I need her. With one word falling over the other, Daniel tried to reassure Lorelei.

"Honey, don't cry, and don't worry, I won't push you. I just want to be with you. I'll wait for you until you're ready to marry me. We're both young enough to postpone a bit. And I know how much your family and business mean to you. What do you say about me transferring to a school down here? That would give us more time to be together. Just say that it's not impossible, sweetheart."

"No, oh no, my darling," Lorelei choked the words out around the tears blocking her throat. "I don't think it's impossible at all. And I don't want to wait to marry you. I just realized that my loving you is never going to change."

"Then let's take a taxi to Tijuana, right now," he exalted.

Wiping her eyes on the handkerchief he gave her, Lorelei managed a rather watery grin. "My folks and Susan would never forgive us if they weren't invited to our wedding. And besides, you had my appetite all primed for that special omelette."

"Damn, I should have remembered that the way to a

woman's heart is through her stomach,'' Daniel said, dramatically hitting his forehead.

Suddenly aware of the looks they were getting from the guard, Lorelei tugged on Daniel's arm, indicating that it was time to leave.

He nodded his agreement, but when they passed the man on their way out the door, Daniel reached for the guard's hand, giving it a hearty shake.

"Congratulate me, my friend, she's finally going to marry me!"

They left the protection of the Wright house and made a dash back to the car.

All through the drive back to her home Lorelei and Daniel discussed the details of their new life together. But even with that fascinating subject to occupy the trip, it seemed endless to Lorelei. Only when she glanced at her watch did she realize that they were caught in rush-hour traffic.

To make matters worse, when they stopped at her neighborhood market to buy supplies for their overdue lunch, it looked to Lorelei as if all the local residents had also decided to stock up on groceries.

It was close to six when they finally pulled into her drive, and Lorelei saw that Tom Sumoto was locking up for the day.

"Hi there, Lori," he called to her when she exited the Nova. "You just missed your sister and brother-in-law. John wanted to take some measurements for the sprinklers, and Susan said that she had something important for you to see. She was going to put it on your kitchen table."

"Thanks, Tom. Have you met Daniel Logan?"

"Sure, Clint introduced him last Saturday. We had a brief chat." He grinned a hello to Daniel.

"And in five minutes, Tom told me everything I'll ever need to know about kapok trees."

"He's the one to ask," Lorelei agreed. "Tom, tell Mioshi to give the baby a kiss for me, and remind her about that shopping spree we're going on to celebrate her new-found waistline."

Tom rolled his eyes heavenward and waved goodbye as he walked toward his truck.

"Great guy you've got there," Daniel commented as he followed Lorelei into the building.

"Yeah, but it's hard to take when your manager knows more than you do about the business."

"Oh, I doubt that there's much you don't know about the nursery, Lori."

"Maybe about the practical day-to-day running of things. But Tom *knows* plants, right down to their molecules. He's done some genetic crosses that promise to yield fantastic new varieties of ferns."

"Well, I hope he doesn't come up with something that looks up and says 'feed me.' " Daniel chuckled and Lorelei joined in.

They were still laughing as she turned on the light in her kitchen. When Lorelei went over to the table to put down a bag of food and her carry-all, she noticed a folded newspaper on the wooden surface.

Attached to the paper was a note. "Lori," it read, "I couldn't get hold of you today, but look what I found at the grocery store this morning. Read the story on page three. I'm sure it's not as bad as it seems. Call me!!!, Susan."

Intrigued, Lorelei unfolded the paper. It was one of those national tattler editions that call to you in the check-out line of the supermarket, promising to reveal strange facts and weird occurrences.

The front page of this one featured evidence that Big Foot had been recruited by the Rams . . . and had a tale about a housewife who grew a squash that formed a picture of Elvis on its skin.

Turning to the third page, Lorelei gasped at the quarter-page picture that jumped out at her. "Oh my god!" she cried. Had she really looked this bad? How had Daniel had the courage to walk into that crowded dining room with her?

"Lori, Lori, what's the matter, sweetheart?" He had come to her side at the sound of her distress.

Lorelei pointed a slender finger at the full-color picture, and then saw the caption. "BEAUTY AND THE . . . Popular model Daniel Logan escorts San Diego local Lorelei Hunt to dinner at the Hotel Ramona."

No need to guess who the editor labeled the beauty here. Daniel looked magnificent in his dinner jacket.

Thanks to Susan's expert make-up, Lorelei seemed to have no features at all. No cheekbones, no chin, and a thin slash of a mouth. The only things that stood out on her face were her eyes, magnified by her glasses and showing a glint of retinal redness through the pale blue of her irises.

Lorelei laughed shakily, "I really put you through a terrible ordeal, didn't I, darling?" She smiled up at Daniel, ready to laugh with him over the joke she had played on herself.

But Daniel wasn't smiling. In fact, his face was utterly grim. His eyes were still focused on the paper.

"Don't be angry, Dan. What editor wouldn't be tempted to publish such a picture of contrasts?"

Daniel still didn't raise his eyes, and it was then that Lorelei noticed that he wasn't looking at the picture; he was reading the column below. For the first time, she realized that a fairly long story accompanied the picture. The article appeared to be a bylined gossip column. Lorelei's eyes widened as she read what Sherman Schreiber had told "Sassy Sadie" about his favorite client.

"Lorelei Hunt, a recent divorcée, sent a fan letter to my client, Daniel Logan, praising his work in the award-winning jeans ad that everybody's been talking about for months.

"Her letter touched us," the quote went on, "and reading between the lines, Daniel Logan realized how lonely she was. Out of the goodness of his big heart, he decided to put a ray of sunshine into Ms. Hunt's life and treat her to a dinner at the glamorous Hotel Ramona."

Why, he was nothing but an opportunistic leech, Lorelei thought to herself, wincing at how Schreiber had twisted the event, making it seem that she had been begging for help and dying to meet Daniel. Lorelei settled into the arm Daniel had placed around her shoulder; it wasn't his fault that his agent was such a slug.

She was about to grab the paper and throw it in the garbage where it belonged when something in the next paragraph caught her eye.

"We talked to Daniel Logan the night of his date with Lorelei Hunt," Sassy Sadie went on, "and he confirmed the facts his agent presented. He also said that, 'Ms. Hunt is a very interesting woman. She has a successful exotic plant nursery and is very knowledgeable in her field.'

"And when we asked him what sort of plant *she* reminded him of, he paused a moment and then said, 'I guess you'd have to say she's like a spiny desert cactus . . . you have to look really hard to see anything attractive . . .' "

A little moan of disbelief escaped Lorelei's throat. She whirled away from Daniel's arm, turning to face the man who stared at her, his features a study in pain.

"Did you say this?" she whispered.

"No! Well . . . not really," he stammered. "Todd Jenkins, who's Sassy Sadie by the way, has taken my words and twisted them out of context. Remember, I spoke to him before dinner, before . . ."

"Before you found out that I wasn't really homely! Now tell me, did you or did you not compare me to a *cactus*!"

"Honey, please read between the lines," Daniel pleaded. "Can't you see by my words that even then I must have known I was falling in love with you, and I didn't care if you were plain or not! Lori, Jenkins left out the most important parts."

"I don't believe you! That's what Howard used to do. He always blamed someone else."

"Lori, now listen to me . . ."

"Oh, I've already listened to you. I've listened to you more than enough. All the hogwash about searching for me, and all those sincere statements about fitting your life into mine."

"But I meant every word I've said."

"Yeah, especially about having to look real hard to see anything attractive about me!"

"Lori, please, it wasn't like that . . ."

"Oh, just shut up. I've had enough experience with a man who could make me believe anything he said. Howard had everybody fooled for years. And you did it, too. And even my family was taken in again. Only Mark saw through you. He warned me about trusting you."

"Yeah, I'll bet he did. And I can understand his motives . . . the poor sap is crazy about you." But not as much as he was, Daniel reminded himself. And recalling Lorelei's experience with her ex-husband, he tried once again to make her see the truth.

"Lori, I didn't try to fool your family. I think they're wonderful. I'd give anything to have parents like your and a sister like Susan. She and John have just the kind of home life I've always wanted."

"Ah hah! So that's the attractive thing you finally found about me . . . my family. That makes sense—you poor little orphan. Marry me and you've got instant mother and father and sister."

"Damn it, you're not making any sense. Listen to me. It's only you I want. I want to be with you, to live with you, to go to school with you . . ."

"School? School! What's the matter, is the tuition at U.C.L.A. getting a little steep for you? Is that why you're planning to move down here? Is that the reason you cozied up to George Tolliver at the picnic? Are you looking for a little high-paying work from him?"

"My God, you don't really think that I need Tolliver's patronage, do you?"

"Oh, yes, I do. Why else would you pull up all your roots in Los Angeles to come down here?"

Daniel couldn't believe this was happening. Were a few hasty words on his part going to ruin his whole life? What else could he say to make her see the truth?

But searching Lorelei's angry face, he suddenly realized that there was *nothing* he could say that would make a difference. Lorelei was looking for a way out. She was still terrified of commitment, and this incident provided her with the perfect solution. Not only did she get out of marrying him, she could also put the blame on his head!

A slow red line of anger moved up his neck.

"There's another explanation for all my actions, but you're too filled with self-pity over what Howard Taylor did to you to understand what I really wanted from you."

"Oh, I know what you wanted from me, and you got it on Sunday," Lorelei yelled at him.

Daniel grabbed her by the shoulders. "Damn it, you little fool. I'm sick and tired of paying for another man's sins. I told you that I am not promiscuous. I have to feel something for the woman I take to my bed. Well, you've just killed everything I felt for you. And, lady, I wouldn't take you again, if you came dancing naked up Wilshire Boulevard to get me.''

Letting go of her, he stalked to the door, turning as he flung it open.

''Goodbye, Lorelei, thanks for everything you've taught me—about San Diego, about exotic plants, and especially about spiny cactuses that prove to be just as ugly in the center as they are on the surface.''

The sound of Daniel slamming the door masked the noise Lorelei made kicking a kitchen chair. ''Damn, that hurts,'' she muttered, the words covering both the state of her foot and that of her heart.

Hobbling over to the sofa, Lorelei sat down and stripped off her sandal. She wiggled her big toe experimentally. It didn't seem to be broken, but the condition of her heart wasn't as easily ascertained.

Well, she had been fooled again, Lorelei thought, squeezing her eyes tight against angry tears. Maybe she shouldn't enter college in the fall—it seemed that she was too stupid to learn from her mistakes. But Daniel had seemed so different from Howard. She had believed that he was too honest to lead her on for his own gain as her ex-husband had done.

Even tonight, when the evidence had been in black and white, Daniel sounded so convincing, so hurt by her accusations. She could still see the pain in his eyes and hear the desperation in his voice.

God, to add to all his other attractions, the man was a consummate actor. But even as that caustic thought surfaced in her brain, Lorelei found herself going over the last fifteen minutes once again.

''Read between the lines,'' he had begged. Limping over to the kitchen table, she picked up the tabloid. On the front page, the headline predicted a major earthquake in Los Angeles . . . based on the authority of a noted pop singer. Another hot item gave a recipe for a guaranteed love potion.

Was this piece of journalistic garbage to be believed over Daniel's frantic denials? Flipping to the notorious story on page three, Lorelei read the column once again. There they were, the three dots Daniel had tried to point out to her. What had he said after that cruel statement? Could it have been something that changed the whole tone of the quote?

Pressing the paper to her breast, Lorelei wrestled with her emotions. How she wanted to believe that she had been wrong! Her hand went to the phone receiver. Daniel would go to Susan's, at least to pick up his suitcase before starting back to Los Angeles.

Maybe she should call her sister and ask her to have Daniel phone when he got there.

The strong, masculine hammering on her door arrested her hand. He had come back! Daniel had not given up on her. He had probably thought of some indisputable fact that would prove he had been telling the truth.

Forgetting the pain in her toe, Lorelei flew to the door and flung it open.

Mark Tolliver stood in the entrance, with an all too familiar tabloid clutched in his hand.

Pushing past her into the room, he waved the paper excitedly. "Lori, wait till you hear what I've found out. Look at this . . . Oh, you've already got one," he said, finally seeing the copy in her own hand.

"Yes, bearer of glad tidings. I've read the delightful story."

"Well, you don't sound too broken up about it. Don't you understand what they've done, that redhead and his agent?"

"Gotten a whole lot of publicity, I imagine," Lorelei

said. "Look, Mark, truthfully, I was upset when I first saw this story. But think about the source. Do you really think we should put too much credence in what this reporter said?"

"How about my father . . . how much credence do you think he has?"

"I don't understand."

"Dad's been out of town, so I just learned an hour ago that Sherman Schreiber called him bright and early on Monday, congratulating him on his new ad agency. The man then went on to extol Daniel Logan, and all his other models, hinting that Dad could do worse than use his clients exclusively for any modeling assignments."

"I still don't understand."

"Don't you see, Lori. Nobody outside our firm was supposed to know about that acquisition. We kept it a secret so that there wouldn't be a run on the stock that would drive up the price before the signing. Think, woman! Schreiber called on Monday . . . the day after the picnic. And I heard Dad mention the ad agency at least half a dozen times at Susan's. Why not? He was with family and trusted friends. And one redheaded opportunist."

Lorelei dropped the tabloid as if it had burst into flames. Blindly staggering over to the couch, she threw herself down on the cushions, and buried her head in a throw pillow, trying to stifle the wretched sobs that shook her body.

Dimly, she heard Mark call her name over and over. But she couldn't answer him. She was too busy mourning the final demise of her sense of trust. Howard had done a number on it, but Daniel's treachery had killed it.

She cried until nothing more came from her tear ducts. When she finally quieted, her throat was sore and scratchy.

It was only then that she noticed the lights had been dimmed, and soft music filled the room.

Struggling to sit up, Lorelei was immediately presented with a warm washcloth and a dry towel. Mark sat next to her while she wiped her tears away. And when she could look up at him with a wobbly little smile of thanks, he put his arm around her shoulders and pulled her head against his chest.

Lorelei sat like that for several minutes, listening to the strong, steady beat of Mark's heart, playing counterpart to the smooth male voice that was coming from her grandfather's old hi-fi set.

One song ended and another began. And when Lorelei recognized "Misty" and its singer, she sat up straighter, looking into Mark's gray eyes.

"I didn't know that you were a secret Johnny Mathis fan," she challenged.

"There's a lot you don't know about me, darling."

Mark's head dipped towards hers, and Lorelei found herself fighting the desire to turn her cheek into the kiss that was coming. But then a sudden thought stopped her. Perhaps a demonstration would be the best explanation of all.

It was a hard, deep, searching kiss—one that delved and explored and went on for long seconds. But when Mark finally raised his head to look into Lorelei's eyes once more, it wasn't passion that darkened his irises.

"You've always known this, haven't you, Lori?" he asked in a quiet voice.

"That the spark wasn't there? Yes, Mark, I guess I have."

"But why? Why not?"

"I really don't know. Maybe that old cliché about chemistry. Our molecules just don't call to each other."

"But I wanted you . . . I really did," Mark protested.

"All these years I've been searching for someone like you. All the time you were Howard's wife and off limits to me, I wanted you desperately."

"Maybe that's the reason . . . I was unavailable to you," Lorelei said softly. "As you said at the picnic, I met Howard just when I was at my most vulnerable, and I never thought about another man until after the divorce."

"When you went gaga over Daniel Logan," he said wryly.

"Well, I'm not mad about the man any more," Lorelei assured Mark with just a tiny catch in her throat. "And I'll survive to live another day."

"I'm glad that you're so strong, Lori. To tell you the truth, until I talked with my dad today, I *really* didn't think there was anything shady about Logan. All that guff I gave you was just me acting like a jealous fool. Too bad. I think I even might have liked the guy, if he could have made you happy."

"Thank you for being so honest, Mark," Lorelei said, patting his hand.

"So, Logan's out of the picture. You're going to start the rest of your life tomorrow . . . and where does this leave us, Lori?" he finally asked.

"As best friends, dear. Friends who would do anything for each other. Anything but make another marital mistake together."

"Well, now that I realize I've been looking in the wrong direction for all these years, what kind of woman do I really want?" Mark leaned his head back against the couch and closed his eyes for a second.

The record player and Johnny Mathis finally gave him his answer. When Mark left Lorelei's apartment a few minutes later, he was whistling "Dark Eyes."

* * *

Pacing in front of the television, Lorelei ignored the first few rings of the phone. But the caller was persistent, and she finally answered the summons.

Susan's note had asked her to call, and this was probably her now. God, she needed to talk to her sister.

"Hello . . . Susan?"

". . . Is this Lorelei Hunt?" The feminine voice definitely was not her sister's.

"Yes, this is she."

"Lori, this is Mattie Dunne . . . remember me? We were in Mr. Kouzoujian's American literature class in our junior year."

"Ah, of course, Mattie, but weren't you Mattie Arnold back then?"

"Yes, but that was three, or maybe four, husbands ago."

"Well, nice to hear from you, Mattie. What can I do for you? Did you want me to order some special plant, or . . ."

"No, Lori. I just wanted to say that if you ever need to talk to someone, don't hesitate to call."

"Talk to someone? To you?" Lorelei had been thinking just that a few seconds ago. But she hadn't had Mattie in mind. She hadn't seen the girl—woman—in ten years.

"My dear, I saw your picture in that awful rag today. I thought I had been through a lot, but when I saw what had happened to your beautiful face . . . Well, divorce can be as bad as an auto wreck on a girl. The things I could tell you about Richard. Richard Farrall, he was my first. And you wouldn't believe what Alan—husband number two—did before I dumped him. Then there was . . ."

"Mattie . . . Mattie, wait! I get the idea," Lorelei broke in. "Thank you for the offer. And if I ever feel in the need, I'll certainly consider giving you a call."

"Well, good. I'll talk to you some more at the reunion on Saturday."

"Reunion . . . oh, it is this Saturday, isn't it? No, I hadn't planned on going, and it's too late to get tickets now," Lorelei said, sending up a special prayer of thanks that the deadline for ordering tickets was last week.

"Oh, that's too bad, we were so anxious to see . . . that is, to help you."

" 'We'?"

"Just some of the girls, the group that kept in touch. We all go to the Hidden Pines spa for a few days each month to work off a couple of pounds and get their special facials. Say, that's an idea . . . you could come, too. Even if you're not going to the reunion, it'll do you all the good in the world. So, what do you say, shall I make a reservation for you to join us sometime?"

"Mattie, I truly appreciate your concern, but let me assure you that I really don't look like the picture you saw. And I'm certainly not grieving over divorcing Howard. I don't have the time. I have a business to run, and a deadline coming up for a book I'm writing. But why don't you give me a call after the reunion and we'll get together for lunch someday?"

"Oh, I'm off to Venice on Sunday, and then there's Greece, that's compliments of Roger, my latest ex. But I will call soon," she promised and rang off.

Lorelei groaned, praying that Mattie encountered husband number four—or was it five?—on her trip and forgot all about doing her bit of "charity work" for Lorelei Hunt.

She suddenly felt very tired. Maybe she'd better try to get some sleep, Lorelei decided. On her way to the bedroom, the phone rang again. It was Cynthia Woods, another high school classmate.

"Lori, I can't believe you were dumb enough to let

Howard do a facelift on you just before the divorce!"
Cynthia began . . . and then she really got brutal.

With her blood pressure threatening to give her apo-
plexy, Lorelei took two more calls from mere acquain-
tances. Each chat was a variation of the conversation she
had had with Mattie and Cynthia. And none of the women
seemed to believe her when she told them that the newspaper photographer had just caught her at a bad angle. They
all sounded crushed when they learned that she wasn't
planning to go to the event of the decade.

Thoroughly disgusted, Lorelei finally pulled the plug on
her phone, deciding not to switch on her answering
machine. She didn't even want to listen to recorded messages from these ghouls. It seemed that a good percentage
of her graduation class had grown up to be the kind of
people who gather at dangerous street crossings, waiting
for gruesome traffic accidents.

For a minute, Lorelei was tempted to crash the gala on
Saturday, just to prove to everyone that nothing had happened to her face. But if she did, she would still have to
endure being in the same room with Howard and Carol.
That meeting probably would give the bloodsucking
alumni enough grist for their gossip mill to last them
another ten years.

Well, there was no way that she was going to give them
the satisfaction.

No way.

THIRTEEN

"Lori, open this door. I know you're inside, so open up," Susan banged on Lorelei's apartment door early Thursday morning.

"OK, OK, hold your horses, I'll be right there," Lorelei called as she finished braiding her shower-damp hair.

"Well, it's about time," Susan said by way of a greeting. "Lori, why didn't you call me last night? I tried and tried, but the phone was always busy. I even had the operator check, and she said it was in use."

"It was at first, but so many people called about the newspaper picture I finally pulled the plug." Lorelei walked over to the instrument and reinserted the attachment to the wall jack.

The phone immediately began ringing. Groaning, she quickly turned on the answering machine, and adjusted the sound to the lowest position. She'd check the call later to see if it was something important, or just another former classmate.

"Well, you turned your phone off, and then they started calling me."

196

"Nice to know that people are so worried about *moi*, isn't it?" Lorelei asked with a wry smile.

"Of course, they are . . . at least some of them are," Susan said. "Lori, what in the world happened between you and Dan? He drove by my house yesterday afternoon to pick up his stuff before going back to L.A. He was in a positive fury. I snatched his car keys and made him swim laps before letting him start back north.

"I couldn't get a thing out of him at first, but then he said something about putting his big foot into his mouth and wanting to kick you in your gorgeous derrière . . . but I don't think he had that exact word in mind."

Lorelei laughed in spite of herself. "Well, the foot in his mouth is what he said in that article. And the kick in my rear was for what I said to him, after I read his quotes and went through the roof. We exchanged some pretty mean words. Wish I had him here again. I've thought of a lot more."

"Lori, you know what these kinds of newspapers are like. Surely he didn't say . . ."

"Oh, but he did. He admitted talking to that reporter at the Hotel Ramona."

"But it's so unlike Dan to say something so cruel."

"Guess it's just another case of the Hunt girls believing a sweet-talking man. First Howard, and now . . ."

"Oh no, he is *nothing* like Howard. You couldn't put another Howard past me without setting off all kinds of alarms and whistles," Susan assured her.

"Well, how do you explain the article? Oh, he tried to get me to believe that he had been quoted out of context. And even if he was telling the truth about that, what about what Mark told me last night?"

Lorelei gave her sister a detailed account of how Sherman Schreiber had called George Tolliver using privileged information . . . information that he must have learned from Daniel Logan.

"And now that I think about it, Daniel's plans to move down here from Los Angeles make more sense . . . he probably wants to be close to the new ad agency," Lorelei concluded.

"Daniel said he was going to move to San Diego?"

"Yes, right after he proposed."

"He asked you to marry him?"

"Susan, has something gone wrong with your hearing? Read my lips. The man has an agenda. He wants to become an architect as quickly as he can. And what better way to make big bucks fast than to get in good with Uncle George and have the pick of the best modeling assignments."

"No, absolutely not. Lori, honey, I don't understand about the quotes in the article. But what was so privileged about knowing the Tollivers' were buying an advertising firm? Uncle George was telling everybody at the picnic about it. I heard him, John heard him . . . I'll bet even Amelia's friend Mary Beth heard him! It could have been one of my neighbors that let the word out."

"But no one else was in a position to gain from that information . . . only Daniel Logan, the user."

"Lorelei Hunt! Bite that wicked tongue of yours. Did you ever stop to think that maybe Sherman Schreiber just has better sources of information than Mark realizes? Don't ever say that Daniel is a user! Why, he wouldn't even stay at our place without paying his way. And I don't mean by making a false show of offering room and board. Instead, he made us the most wonderful dinner the night he stayed with us. After your expedition, he stopped for all the ingredients and then had John and me relax out by the pool while he cooked."

"Daniel cooked your dinner?"

"Gourmet-class meal. And he did everything himself, except for getting the kids to help set the table and wash up afterwards. Then he sat up for hours, improving upon the rough designs he did for your new greenhouse sprinkler system."

"Oh, no!" Lorelei gasped.

"Oh, yes. As I said, Lori, the man pays his way. And I've never seen anyone who loves family life as much as Daniel Logan."

"Of course, he appreciates your family. That's another one of my attractions. He's never had one of his own and I have this wonderful, ready-made clan for him."

"Lori!" Susan admonished. "You don't really think that."

Lorelei felt tears of shame prick her eyes. "No, Susan, I guess that I don't really believe Daniel would pursue me because of my family. Seems that my experience with Howard has warped my judgment. God, how could I keep reminding Dan that he was an orphan? That's the most awful thing I've ever said to anyone. No matter what Daniel said to the reporter, or to Schreiber, I never should have retaliated with that kind of low blow."

Susan held her arms out to her taller sister as Lorelei started to sob. Lorelei was too upset to interpret the look of satisfaction on the older woman's face as she went into Susan's arms.

"Lori, it's all going to work out," Susan said, patting her sister's back. "He loves you, you love him. Nothing else matters."

"No, Suzie, it's over," Lorelei said, her voice thick with tears. "He'll never forgive the awful things I accused him of. Could you keep loving someone who has no faith in you?"

"Lori, now stop. Wipe your face and listen to me. I have to tell you about one of the calls I got yesterday.

Who do you think phoned me when she couldn't get through to you?''

"Who?" Lorelei asked, blowing her nose with the tissue Susan provided.

"The new Mrs. Howard Taylor. The ever lovely Carol."

"What did that bimbo want?" Lorelei sniffed.

Susan laughed. "She'd seen the newspaper, of course. And she said that she just was devastated at the thought of how much pain losing Howard has caused you. The dear heart offered to pay for a month at a resort, a new wardrobe . . . and even for the psychiatric counseling you need to get back on your feet."

"Psychiatric counseling! She's the one who needs help with that twisted little mind of hers. Do you know that she stalked Howard for over eight years? It seemed sad at the time, so I never told anybody, but every time Howard and I went anywhere—to a show, or to dinner—there Carol would be, in the next row or at the next table.

"She even invited herself over a few times, before I realized what was going on. She brought these strange little presents. Howard used to say she was a pitiful basket case . . . right up to the day it dawned on him how he could become a partner in her father's plastic surgery clinic."

Lorelei felt like smashing something at the thought that Carol Taylor felt sorry for *her*. "Lord, if there were only some way I could get back at her," she raged at Susan. "Some way to prove to her that she's welcome to the slug she's married."

"There is, dear. You can pay her back, and lay low those other wonderful people who've been trying to find out about your troubles. All you have to do is go to the reunion."

"I thought about doing that, but it's impossible. The reunion is in two days and it's too late to get a ticket."

"Uh-uh." Susan shook her head. "There were a few last-minute cancellations, and Carol was more than willing to reserve a pair of tickets for you. They'll be waiting at the reception desk at the banquet hall. I already told her that you were coming with the gorgeous model in the newspaper photograph."

"Daniel? Oh, Susan, Daniel would never come with me after the way I treated him."

"Oh yes, he will. I called him just before I came over here. The man may have an awful temper, but it seems that he cools off quickly. He jumped at the chance to see you again. He said he's got some important work to do, so he can't get here before Saturday, but he'll pick you up then at seven o'clock. The rest is up to you, sweetie pie. But I'm sure that, with Daniel by your side, you'll have no difficulty devastating every one of those small-minded classmates who called . . . not to mention ruining Carol Taylor's whole evening!"

As Susan put away the make-up, Lorelei looked at her face in the hand-held mirror she used to check her sister's progress. Déjà vu, but with such a difference!

Instead of the wan, undefined features Susan had created last week, now every one of Lorelei's good points had been enhanced and highlighted. She felt that she had never looked more beautiful.

"Thank you, Susan. If nothing else, this face will give me the confidence to deal with everybody tonight." Everybody except Daniel, she thought. The first part of the evening would be the hardest.

"Let's get you into your dress, what there is of it," Susan suggested.

"You don't think it's too daring?" Lorelei asked.

Yesterday afternoon she had gone on a whirlwind shopping spree with Susan, and had fallen in love with the designer knock-off. But she suddenly felt afraid that it was absolutely wrong for her.

"It's a wonderful dress," Susan assured her. "I just wish I were half a foot taller. I'd borrow it from you and send John's blood pressure into the stratosphere."

In her bedroom, Lorelei took the spangled black creation off its hanger. With Susan's help, she slipped the halter-topped gown over her head. The front was demure, with a choker collar. The full sensual impact of the dress became evident only when she turned around, revealing that its back started well below her waist.

It was also obvious that only a lacy garter belt and bikini pants could escape detection in the cut of that dress.

After slipping into slender-strapped shoes with matching glitter, Lorelei gave her hair one last brushing. The expert stylist she visited yesterday had cut thick bangs, but only shortened the length of her hair a bit by blunting the ends. The result was a golden Cleopatra-inspired style that felt carefree and utterly chic.

"Dan's going to be very busy keeping the other fellas from fogging up your contacts," Susan offered as she gave Lorelei two thumbs up.

"Are you sure that I'm doing the right thing?" Lorelei found herself asking once more.

"Absolutely . . . you'll knock them dead, kiddo."

"No, I mean about seeing Daniel again."

"I won't even grace that with an answer. Oh, oh, he's here," Susan cocked her ear to the sound of knocking downstairs. "Caught in the act again. I'll just wait up here and let myself out after you're gone."

Lorelei wanted to drag her sister along and use her as a buffer. But with a brave, rather wobbly smile, she picked up her purse and went down.

When the door opened, Daniel took a step forward, and then froze in the frame. This had better be Lorelei, he thought, or I'm in serious trouble. His custom-fitted trousers were not designed to handle the instantaneous reaction this lovely creature had provoked.

Daniel was larger than she remembered, Lorelei thought, looking up at the man in her doorway. Larger and taller . . . and absolutely breathtaking in his perfectly cut dinner jacket. She felt sure she would have to fight off predatory women tonight, not that she could really blame them.

"Lori?" he murmured, sounding unsure. "Lori, you're m-magnificent, I-I . . ." He stuttered to a stop, unable to control his tongue.

A warm, wonderful feeling welled up in Lorelei. She knew that she looked good tonight, but the stunned expression in Daniel's eyes was all that really mattered. Without another word, she smiled up at him and slipped her hand into his. They walked out to his waiting Corvette. Once they were both inside the car, Daniel turned to her.

"Sweetheart, can you ever . . ." he began, but Lorelei reached over to silence him with gentle fingers pressed to his lips.

"Before you say anything, Daniel, please open the present I have for you," she said in a small voice.

"A present?" He looked bemused, and then aghast. "Oh, my God. Is it a boutonniere? Lorelei, I forgot to get you a corsage! How could I have forgotten?" he groaned, smacking his forehead with the flat of his palm.

"The same way I forgot to get you a boutonniere," Lorelei laughed. "It's because we've had a lot more important things on our minds during the last few days."

She held out a small, brightly wrapped package. "This is my present. Go on, open it up,' she urged, when he just turned it over and over in his large hands.

Carefully separating the paper, Daniel finally held up

the rectangular object that had been inside. He examined all sides of it, and then chuckled. "My very own Frank Lloyd Wright eraser. Lori, this is wonderful. Where did you get it?"

"I went back to the art museum this morning. Knowing how much the man's work means to you, I hoped they would have something about the Usonian exhibit in the gift shop—maybe a poster or a photo. But when I saw this, I thought it would be the perfect peace offering."

Daniel's bronze-colored eyes were shining with pleasure as he leaned forward to kiss her. But Lorelei stopped him, putting her hand on his arm.

"Wait, darling. It's hard enough to think with you so near, but if you kiss me, I'm lost. And I have to say my piece before I die of shame."

"Lori, sweetheart, there isn't any need . . ."

"But there is," she insisted. "Dan, I was hoping that you would use this eraser to rub away from your memory all the insulting things I've said to you during the last week. Please forgive me for throwing your background at you, and for accusing you of being a user . . . like the person I refuse to mention tonight. I never really believed you were like him. I guess I just had to purge the last bit of the anger I had inside me, and unfortunately, you got the brunt of it."

"It's all forgotten. The unmentionable man, the things you said to me, and the stupid things I said to that reporter. He did quote me accurately . . . as far as he went. But I already told you about those three little dots at the end of the sentence?"

Lorelei nodded, letting him have his say.

"What I didn't have a chance to tell you the other night was that he didn't put in the part that said, though you were like a spiny desert cactus, when I looked carefully, I found a beautiful soul shining through, and someone I wanted as my friend. And, Lori . . . there's something else you should know . . . something I just found out about this morning.''

"Something about a certain call our dear friend Sherman made to George Tolliver?" Lorelei said with a grin. "Mark told me about it. He was sure you gave your agent insider information."

"You knew? God, Lori . . . you didn't think . . . didn't . . .'' Daniel stopped and then took a deep breath before speaking again. "Darling, I didn't say anything to Sherman about the ad agency . . . he had his own sources of information. But I did tell him in very blunt language what he could do with any assignment involving the Tolliver firm."

"But, Daniel . . .''

"No, Lorelei, I'd never trade on a friendship, and now Sherman knows that, too. The idea of me modeling for the Tolliver agency is a closed subject. I just wanted you to be aware of what happened, because I never want a misunderstanding or misdirected anger to drive us apart again. I felt like the living dead after I left you Wednesday evening, and I never want to experience that pain again. Is that understood?" he questioned with a mock sternness that still rang with firm resolve.

When Lorelei just nodded meekly, Daniel laughed and said, "While I may have forgotten your corsage, I do have a couple of presents for you. I meant to give them to you after the reunion, but this may be a better time."

He reached forward and, for the first time, Lorelei realized that there was a long tube on the dashboard. Daniel uncapped the metal end and drew forth a sheath of blueprint paper.

When he handed it to her, Lorelei slowly scanned the first page, realizing that it was a beautifully detailed schematic for her greenhouse sprinkler system. The rest of the pages were exploded views of various details.

"This is why I couldn't get here before today," Daniel explained. And the look that was on Lorelei's face when she raised her head made the two twenty-hour days he had spent on the project well worth it.

"Daniel, I don't know what to say."

"Your eyes told everything I needed to know about the plans," he said as he replaced them in the tube. "But I *do* want to hear your exact reaction to this." In his hand was a small, square box.

Opening it with shaking fingers, Lorelei moaned when she saw the perfect diamond glittering in dark blue velvet.

"It's a beautiful ring, Daniel . . . I love it. But not nearly as much as I love you."

"Thems the right words," he drawled with satisfaction. "Then you'll accept it? Accept me . . . marriage, and everything?"

"Did you ever have any doubt of it?" Lorelei whispered, and then laughed softly at the groan of disbelief that rose out of Daniel's long throat.

But when she held out her hand, she sighed happily as he carefully slid the symbol of his enduring love in place.

"I'll have that kiss now," Daniel said, leashed need roughening his voice.

It felt just like the first time he kissed her, Lorelei thought, as his lips tested softly, and then hardened when her mouth opened to his command. The tip of his tongue touched hers in a brief salute. But with a harsh intake of breath, he then plunged deeply, wreaking soft carnage over the delicate tissues, until Lori found herself tugging at his jacket. She tried to find the buttons of his shirt, desperate to feel the heat of his skin under her fingers.

But before she loosened even the first button, Daniel grabbed her hands, stilling their frantic search. Fighting for control, he chuckled hoarsely into her ear. "Well, Cinderella, the ball awaits, and if we don't leave now, we'll never get you there in time to fill up your dance card."

"Wouldn't bother me a bit," she countered, trying to cool the blood raging through her body.

"Well, let's just put in an appearance . . . I understand from Susan that there are a few of your former classmates that I should meet." The tinge of menace in his voice startled her for a second.

But then he reached over to snap Lorelei's seatbelt, and ran a lingering hand over her shoulder. Daniel hesitated before guiding his fingers in a long journey down her bare back.

"Oh, my God," he suddenly breathed. "On second thought, forget what I said about filling your dance card. I'll be damned if you go into anyone else's arms tonight."

As Lorelei softly laughed at his outraged possessiveness, Daniel snapped his own harness together and twisted the key in the ignition.

They arrived at the banquet hall only fashionably late. Lorelei gave her name to the volunteer at the door, and he handed them an envelope containing their identification badges and dinner-table assignments.

Inside, Lorelei and Daniel found the proper room, a large rectangular chamber, with a no-host bar at one short end, and the VIP's table at the other. Round tables formed an arc around the dance floor, with a five-piece band completing the circle.

Their numbered table was empty. The other couples were probably circulating or out on the dance floor, Lorelei guessed, as she laid her purse on the tablecloth and pinned on her laminated badge. It had her maiden name, thank God, and her graduation picture.

"Could you pin this on for me?" Daniel asked after fumbling with his own name tag for a moment. "I never seem to get these things on straight."

"Here, I'll do it." Lorelei accepted the badge, and then took a look at it when it was in place. Someone—Carol, no doubt—had found the beautiful wildcat ad, reduced its size, and pasted it on next to Daniel's name.

"Nine-months' pregnant or not, that lady deserves a kick in the . . ." she raged until Daniel's fingers closed around her trembling hands.

"Lorelei, it doesn't matter. Just think of it as a joke . . . a pretty funny joke on me for ever accepting that dumb assignment."

"Oh, Dan, I think it was your sense of the ridiculous that first made me realize that I loved you. What a wonderful trait to pass on to our children."

"Well, if I had known that was all it took, I'd have invested in a joke book," Daniel said.

"Oh, no need to go out and buy one. Just ask my father to loan you something from his collection. He's addicted to puns and shaggy dog stories. Which reminds me, before tonight is over, you are going to tell me exactly what happened between you and this little kitty-cat." She gave the picture on Daniel's badge a little pat.

Throwing his head back, Daniel laughed his delight. At the hoarsely attractive sound, several pairs of eyes homed in on them, and Lorelei suddenly felt apprehensive. What would happen when she saw Howard and Carol?

Instantly understanding the haunted look that had come into her face, Daniel's large hands closed over hers. "There's nothing to be worried about, sweetheart. You're the most beautiful woman in all of San Diego tonight. And I'm very proud of you. Just remember, I'll be at your side all the time."

He brushed his lips on her temple. Lorelei closed her

eyes for an instant, as the warm glow of her love for him burned through her body. She knew that it blazed forth when she opened her eyes again and looked into his beloved face.

"Then I have nothing to fear, do I, Daniel?"

The flare of heat that reflected back from him almost undid Lorelei. She wanted to forget about the party, grab his hand, and find some secret place where she never would have to let him go again.

"I think they're playing our song," Daniel whispered. "Let's dance, Lori."

It was just like the first time they held each other at the Hotel Ramona. "The Lamp is Low" flowed around and over them. Their bodies meshed and their steps synchronized as they moved to Ravel's modernized theme.

As the band played on, Lorelei and Daniel purposely avoided the clumps of graduates who slapped each other on the back and exchanged exaggerated stories of how successful they had become. Daniel seemed familiar with every traditional step and the newest fads. And in his arms, Lorelei picked up the movements she didn't know with incredible ease. They were laughing and out of breath by the time they collapsed in their seats for dinner.

Seven pairs of eyes went wide as the two of them completed the seating arrangement. Husbands turned to wives, and in that silent communication that grows through the years, they clearly said, "I thought you told me that Lorelei Hunt just had a disfiguring accident and was in the middle of a nervous breakdown."

Daniel squeezed Lorelei's hand under the table, and she squeezed back. "Daniel, let me get the introductions started," Lorelei said as she carefully looked at their dinner companions, searching for the teens she had known in the unfamiliar adult faces.

"Well, to your right are Jesse Carter and his wife, the

former Arlene Martin.'' The man nodded, while the woman gave Daniel a slightly dazed smile.

Lorelei went on to present the two other couples, before turning to the woman who had come as a single.

''And last but not least, we have Mattie,'' Lorelei smiled across the table. ''Mattie, it's good to see you again. This is Daniel Logan. Daniel, I'd like to introduce Mattie Arnold Farrall Ginsberg Dunne.''

Lorelei had trouble not laughing hysterically when she read Mattie's badge. Her complete name sounded like a firm of lawyers or accountants! Lorelei wondered why in the world Mattie wanted her whole marital history on her name tag. Maybe getting married three times in the last ten years was her only accomplishment.

''Lori, I see that you managed to get a date. And I'm so glad that you're looking almost normal again,'' she purred. ''How kind of you to bring her, Daniel.

Lorelei ran her nails along Daniel's thigh, silently telling him that the cat in his picture might have been declawed, but the one across the table was not.

''Mattie, Daniel's not my date, he's my fiancé.'' Lori held up her left hand and let the sparkling stone shoot a laser of perfect white light into the woman's eyes. ''Mattie is off to Italy tomorrow. Venice, wasn't it?''

''Venice? Great town, Venice,'' he said, tickling Lorelei's palm with a long finger. ''Nothing beats it during the season. Maybe on your next trip you'll be able to schedule it then.''

Mattie the cat was down to eight lives, Lorelei decided.

Lorelei was fascinated by how creatively Daniel deflected every predatory overture the woman made to him throughout the meal. Only Lorelei seemed to hear the mild disgust in his voice.

Daniel was perfectly charming to everyone else at the table. But he only danced with Lorelei, and she refused every other man's request. They were dancing to something soft and slow when Daniel suddenly pulled her even tighter to his body.

"Oops, sorry about that," a high feminine voice giggled.

"Excuse me, got my feet tangled there for a second," the woman's partner apologized with a laugh. Then everyone but Daniel gasped in surprise when he turned Lorelei so the pair could see her . . . and she could see them.

FOURTEEN

"Lorelei! Lori?"

Dr. Howard Taylor leaned forward around his pregnant wife's ample form to peer into Lorelei's face. "It is you! Carol, why didn't you tell me Lori was going to be here?"

Lorelei took a quick step back into Daniel's arms. The pungent cloud of alcohol from her ex-husband's breath actually made her sick for a second. He was halfway drunk, she realized. Howard's light brown eyes had a blurry cast and his sandy hair needed combing.

"Oh, Lori, dear Lori, you did make it," Carol cooed, ineffectively pushing at the spiky black hair that kept falling over her pale blue eyes.

Lorelei hoped for the sake of the baby Carol was carrying that she hadn't imbibed as much as her husband.

"Howard, I'm sure I told you that Lori might be here if she could get herself a date at the last minute," Carol was saying. "Why don't you introduce us, Lori?"

And for the first time, Carol really looked at the man holding Lorelei. Narrowing her eyes, as if to focus better, she suddenly gave a startled little cry.

Lorelei felt like doing the same thing when she saw Daniel's face.

Cold, graven, perfect, "The Look" was back.

Daniel examined the couple with glacial disdain. These were the people who had caused his Lorelei so much pain and anguish. Remembering his vow to rearrange Taylor's nose, Daniel mentally measured the distance between his fist and the short, snubbed feature centered in that boyish, dissipated face.

His body must have conveyed his intent to Lorelei, because he suddenly became aware that her hand was squeezing his with surprising strength. But when he turned to look at her, laughter danced in her eyes. And then he realized what had happened. Lorelei had let go of her ghosts and she was truly his.

Seeing Daniel's features relax back into their normal warm perfection told Lorelei that he understood what she finally knew—that she had been dreading this encounter for nothing, and that the Taylors could never hurt her in any way again.

Daniel's answering grin made Carol gasp once more, but this time Lorelei saw a sharp, predatory look cross the woman's face.

"Lori, aren't you going to introduce us to your . . ."

"Of course," Lorelei interrupted. "Daniel, this is Carol Taylor and her husband, Howard. Doctor and Mrs. Taylor, this is my fiancé, Daniel Logan."

Lorelei saw the blood drain from Carol's skin as her eyes flew to the perfect diamond on Lorelei's ring finger. It was obvious that Carol's feelings of superiority had received a serious blow, as the pregnant woman's knuckles whitened on her husband's arm.

Howard's complexion ran the gamut of red tones, from baby pink to bright scarlet, Lori noticed. He hadn't taken the news of her engagement any better.

Carol finally released her death grip on Howard's bicep and looked carefully at Lorelei. "I don't understand. Susan said you two were dating. But what about that article in the paper . . . the picture? And, Lori, you look beauti . . . ah, just fine, tonight. But in that picture . . ."

"A bad camera angle," Daniel broke in. "Happens all the time in modeling. You should see some of my reject photos . . . they're absolutely hilarious."

And chickens will grow teeth the same day Daniel Logan photographs badly, Lorelei thought, her heart ready to burst with love for this gorgeous man.

"Oh, yes, the article said that you're a top model," Carol gushed. "Come dance with me, Daniel. I've got so many questions to ask you, about . . . about your modeling. Did you know that I was the one who found this picture of you with your mountain lion?"

Daniel looked between Lorelei and the short, very pregnant woman. Carol was rubbing the top of her stomach, almost as if she were in pain. With a raised eyebrow he communicated to Lorelei that perhaps it would be better to dance with the lady and forestall a premature birth. When Lorelei's mouth twitched her permission, Daniel turned back to Carol.

"May I have this dance?" he asked.

"Howard, why don't you go talk to the principal's wife about that liposuction she mentioned at dinner?" Carol loudly called over her shoulder, as Daniel danced off with her.

Lorelei watched a few seconds as he maneuvered across the floor, trying to keep a respectable distance from Carol's most prominent feature.

Still smiling at the sight, Lorelei was turning to go back to her table when Howard harrumphed at her side. She had actually forgotten that he was there.

"Well, Lorelei, you're looking fabulous . . . never

lovelier. Congratulations on the little farce you staged, great way to save face. But you didn't have to rent the sparkler on your finger or pay for the escort. We'd have been glad to pick you up and take you home."

Lorelei's mouth fell open at Howard's incredible assessment of the situation. "Howard, I see that you're still a slimy slug. Why don't you go crawl back under your rock?" she said in a sweet voice.

"Ah, Lori, come dance with me." He held out his arms, as if he hadn't heard the insult.

Lorelei shrank back, "Not in this lifetime or the next, Howard. I wouldn't let you touch me again if I were drowning in the deep, dark ocean." She nimbly moved around the man and walked away from him.

"Lori, don't be like this," he whined, following her to the edge of the dance floor. "I've been meaning to call you. I've been thinking a lot about you and the divorce. That lawyer of mine was too rough on you. He wouldn't let me give you the settlement I wanted."

That lie was one too many! Lorelei whirled to face her ex-husband again. "Howard, maybe along with the liquor you've drunk tonight, you've also been breathing in too much anesthetic during your operations."

Lorelei didn't care that people around them were staring as she went on. "Don't you remember the phone conversations we had about settlements and alimony? You warned me what would happen if I tried to get a penny from you. I, on the other hand, told you not to worry, that I didn't want a thing from you, except never to see you again."

"Now, Lori, just listen. I admit that I was wrong, I probably should have seen to it that you had enough money to finish your schooling like you always wanted. After all, you did help me with mine in the beginning."

"Beginning! Howard, I paid your tuition for all of medical school, and kept us in clothes and food during your internship. And when you finally were making something in your residency, you took the money I had saved for school and went out to buy yourself a sailboat!"

"Lori, Lori . . . the past is past. Let me make it up to you now." His eyes wandered over to where Daniel Logan danced with the bloated Carol. Howard's gaze returned to Lorelei, examining her slim curves with male appreciation.

"Make it up to me? What are you saying?"

"I'm saying . . ." He suddenly lowered his voice to a whisper. ". . . I'm saying that I've made a great mistake in marrying Carol. I was a fool to give up what we had . . . the lovemaking, the outings together, the lovemaking. Please let me be with you and support you through school."

"Howard. Didn't you hear what I said before? I'm engaged to be married to Daniel Logan. We love each other. And beyond being kind and intelligent, and the most beautiful man I've ever seen, *he* is a fine human being. When I saw you tonight, I remembered that you are as trustworthy as a vulture, and have the morals of a goat. In fact, it's hard to believe you might belong to the same species as Daniel."

"Lori! You don't mean what you're saying. Remember all the good times we had? It could be like that again. I could come over to your apartment, oh, two, three times a week. It could be like the old days."

"Oh, you mean like the time you took the rent money and bought yourself a cashmere sweater? Or the time you got my grandfather in trouble when he cosigned the loan on your car and you didn't make payments for three months? Or maybe you mean the time you told Carol on the phone that she didn't have to worry about being pregnant with your child? You were going to trash me and marry her. Are those the good times you mean, Howard?"

"Well, well . . . well," he said, his mouth gaping.

Lorelei threw back her head and laughed at the stupid expression on his face. "Oh, Howard, I am *so* glad to be rid of you," she finally sputtered. "And you don't have to pay for my education . . . knowing you has been one."

"Howard? What is she saying? Howard!" Carol demanded.

Lorelei hadn't seen Daniel escort the woman off the dance floor, or realized that Carol had heard the last part of her denunciation.

"It's nothing, my sweet," Howard declared with a hearty chuckle. "I was just telling Lori that we'd be glad to loan her some money for her college tuition. But she said we should use it to set up a trust fund for the baby." He placed a placating kiss on Carol's cheek, and then looked over at Lorelei with desperate fear in his eyes.

Ever the weasel, Lorelei thought. But what would she gain by telling Carol that her husband was still an unfaithful lout? The woman would learn that soon enough, Lorelei guessed.

Putting a compassionate hand on Carol's rounded shoulder, Lorelei said, "Have a healthy baby, Carol. I'm sure you and Howard are looking forward to all the joys of parenthood. Now, won't you excuse us? Dan and I have to say hello to some other people."

"Yes," Daniel broke in, looking down on Lorelei with admiration and pride lighting his expressive eyes. "But first Lorelei and I are going out to the patio for a bit of fresh air, and to discuss making some babies of our own."

The traditional reunion activities had begun inside the banquet hall. People were clapping as the couple with the most children and the man with the least hair were identified.

But outside on the patio, Daniel and Lorelei ignored the

laughter. Finding a secluded alcove, Daniel sat down on a low brick wall and pulled Lorelei into his lap.

Without a word he captured her mouth, driving out the soiled feeling her conversation with Howard had generated.

Daniel's hands caressed her shoulders and moved over her bare back. His touch lit a fire of need that coursed down to lick around the very center of her womanly essence.

Finally breaking apart on the brink of complete abandon, Lorelei sucked in several calming breaths before taking Daniel's face between her hands.

"You are so decent, so clean, so moral. Please forgive me for ever confusing your motives with those of that piece of garbage we met in the ballroom. Daniel, there's nothing on earth I'll ever want more than to be your wife."

"Lorelei, my beautiful bride-to-be," he said, taking her in his arms. "I can't wait for us to be together all the time. I want to do so much for you. It'll be so good working and studying together. On Monday, I'll arrange to transfer my credits to U.C. San Diego, and then I'll pay our tuition for the fall semester."

"*Our* tuition?" Lorelei said in a bemused voice. "There's no need to pay for my tuition, Daniel. I'll have enough. There's the book, and my business. Tom has asked to buy in as a partner, which I think is a wonderful idea . . . so my schooling money is taken care of."

"Great, but why don't you save it?" Daniel suggested. "Lori, you don't realize just how much money I'll make from this year's modeling." He named a figure that made her gasp. He would have enough to pay for both his and her tuition for the next *ten* years.

"Well, I'm glad you're all set and can concentrate on your studies, Dan. But how can I let you pay my way, when I resented financing Howard through medical school?"

"Now, Lori. No wife of mine . . ." Daniel began and then stopped short.

Lorelei looked into his eyes—those expressive hazel eyes—and read the solution to their impasse.

"We'll pool our resources," they said in unison.

Daniel laughed. "Such an adult decision. Well, I guess this just proves that I've finally grown up during this last week."

"Yes," Lorelei breathed. "I have, too."

Tears were falling down Lorelei's cheeks. She scrubbed at them, unmindful of the carefully applied make-up her sister had worked so hard over. "I don't know why I'm crying. I'm so very happy," she complained.

Daniel chuckled into her hair. "I feel just the same way, Lori. You make me so happy I want to cry, and laugh, and let everyone know that I love you. When can I let everyone know that I love you? When can we set the date?"

"Just as soon as you tell me about this tom cat here," she sniffed, flicking a fingernail against the photo on his name badge.

"Ah, Lori, it's too embarrassing," Daniel protested.

"Daniel, you promised at the picnic to tell your future wife. And if you don't tell me . . ." Lorelei began a mock threat.

"OK, OK, I guess you should know all about my sordid past. To begin with, this creature isn't a male . . . the little lady is called Tinker Bell. And, well, it seems that she developed a crush on me. Followed me everywhere on location, purred around my ankles, and generally let it be known that she was available." He chuckled, and then took both of Lorelei's hands in his.

"But since I knew she wasn't the girl I'd been waiting

for, I'm ashamed to say that I cruelly spurned her advances.''

''Oh, Dan, I've always known that beast was in love with you . . . you only had to look in its eyes.'' Lorelei laughed, which was a big mistake, because she couldn't stop. Daniel finally put an end to her uncontrolled mirth with a deep, searching kiss.

''Now, tell me, love of my life, when are we going to get married?''

''Just as soon as we can get a judge or a minister. And just as soon as I can invite my family and your . . . Oh, Daniel . . .''

''I'll ask Sherman Schreiber to be my best man,'' he interrupted as tears again formed in Lorelei's eyes at the reminder of how alone he had been.

''Then we'll have to have a kosher caterer for the reception,'' she said with a watery smile. ''Because I'm going to order a whole stack of crunchy matzo for that man to eat!''

EPILOGUE

Daniel tipped the bellboy after the man carried the suitcases into the room and opened the balcony doors.

"Thank you, sir! Will there be anything else, sir?"

"No, we're all set," Daniel said, holding the door open for the man. He locked it after the Hotel Ramona's employee and then turned to Lorelei. Brushing a few grains of rice out of her hair, he said, "It was a wonderful wedding, wasn't it?"

"Yes, everybody had a great time, except maybe Mark. Who would have thought that Sherman Schreiber would have such a beautiful daughter. Mark certainly looked smitten with Rachael, although he told me he'd written off tall blondes."

"Well, I don't think Rachael was equally impressed. What was it that she called him . . . a *schlemazel*?"

"Something like that. I wonder if it's as bad as being a *matzopunim*?"

"I asked Sherman," Daniel said as he pulled off his tie. "He said it means someone who's a lightweight."

"Oh, poor Mark. But good for her! Sounds like Rachael

could run him a good race if she wanted to," Lorelei laughed as she stepped out of her high heels. "These shoes were not made for dancing. But wasn't it was wonderful of Sherman to hire the three-piece band for the reception? I guess, as you said, that he's a good guy after all. Why don't we make it a tradition to hire a band for all of our anniversaries?"

"The first of a long line of Logan family traditions." Daniel sighed happily, taking Lorelei into his arms.

They looked into each other's faces glowing in the light of the setting sun. Linking arms, they walked through the open balcony doors.

The sea below had turned to liquid gold. Lorelei pointed into the sunset, shading her eyes. "Look, you can just see the Point Loma lighthouse."

"Ah, yes, I see it," Daniel agreed, as he lifted his new wife into his arms and walked toward the bed. " 'Build thee more stately mansions, O my soul,' " he quoted once again.

" 'Leaving thine outgrown shell by life's unresting sea,' " Lorelei finished for him, having finally remembered the ending of the poem—now, at the threshold of their new beginning.